THE SEVEN BLACK
CHESSMEN

THE SEVEN BLACK
CHESSMEN

JOHN HUNTINGDON
(GERALD WILLIAM PHILLIPS)

COACHWHIP PUBLICATIONS
Greenville, Ohio

The Seven Black Chessmen, by John Huntingdon
© 2025 Coachwhip Publications edition
Cover image: © GHPhotog

First published 1928
Pseudonym for Gerald William Phillips, 1884-1956
CoachwhipBooks.com

ISBN 1-61646-597-2
ISBN-13 978-1-61646-597-1

I

The Car in the Avenue

At six o'clock on the morning of March the 12th—a day which I have every reason to remember—I emerged from the "White Hart Hotel" at Luttercombe, a little village on the Welsh border. The road was clean and dry, and the grass glistened with dew in the sunlight, though in the shadow of trees or stacks it was still grey with light rime. The morning was not, however, really cold; indeed it was a morning exactly suited to my purpose, which was to fish (by permission indirectly obtained) in private waters, the property of Professor Cheney, and to return after an hour or so with an appetite for the breakfast provided at my not very inviting inn. My next move would be to seek pleasanter quarters.

Idleness and ease were of the essence of my holiday programme, and I strode along without paying any particular attention to the landscape until I found myself at the entrance gates of Cheney Park. Here the road went winding to the left through a wood; and the drive, which I intended to follow, went on through the park. On both sides the trees were tall and thick, and once past the gates I felt a chill in the air. The drive continued for a short distance, and then, curving to the right, led me to a perfectly straight stretch of about half a mile, and so to a slope at the bottom of which I hoped to find my fishing ground.

And here my singular adventure began, for just over the brow of the hill I saw a black unmoving object, which presently proved to be the top of a car with an all-weather body. It was standing in the middle of the road. As I came alongside I could not refrain from giving it a curious glance. What I saw brought me to an abrupt halt. I had expected, seeing no sign of human life, to find the car empty, temporarily deserted; but there was a man seated at the wheel. He sat quite motionless, apparently asleep. Something in his attitude made me look more closely. With growing alarm I peered through the rather dim, narrow windows. The man did not return my scrutiny. I tapped vigorously on the pane. The man did not move.

Wasting no more time I turned back towards the village to get help. It was evident to me that the man was either dead or in a state of coma, and without expert guidance I could do nothing more useful than give the alarm. The church clock chimed a quarter to seven as I re-entered the village, and I made straight for the "White Hart" in the hope that some one there would put me at once on the track of a doctor. As I came within sight of the place I saw Horton Forbes in a dark hat and a dark caped coat entering it from another direction. Even in my rather flustered condition it occurred to me to wonder what on earth the fellow had been up to. Horton Forbes was the only other guest at the "White Hart," and I had met him for the first time on the previous evening. I had been instantly impressed by the force and the queerness of his personality, and astonished when he told me, in a voice full of charm, that he was an insurance agent. But that astonishment had been mild compared with what I felt at sight of him now. I remembered how at about ten o'clock the previous evening Forbes, gradually unfolding himself from his chair like a nonchalant snake, had stemmed the tide of my loquacity by remarking:

"Well, I'll be off to bed. I shall have a pretty busy day to-morrow. I must get some rest while I can."

"I hope," said I, "I haven't bored you too much."

"Far from it, my dear sir," he answered. "I should be delighted to continue our charming conversation almost indefinitely, if I were free, but 'stronger things restrain.' And you know the proverb, 'An opportune future will render protracted toil unnecessary.' Hence my haste."

Saying which he had looked down on me with an air of great benevolence. I did not know the proverb, but I replied:

"Well, I hope we shall meet at breakfast."

"I hope so too," he said; "but it will have to be eightish. I shall leave at nine."

And now here he was, at the ungodly hour of 6.45 a.m., returning with full equipment—I am not sure even that he was not carrying a small bag, though being an unobservant person, I didn't really notice—and looking for all the world as if he had been out a long time, and a long way as well.

All this passed quickly through my mind, for there was no time or occasion to concern myself about it at the moment; and, leaving Forbes to his own devices, whatever they might be, I hurried into the hotel to find the proprietor. Nobody was visible in any of the public rooms, which were still unswept and ungarnished, and reeking of stale tobacco and beer; and it was not until I had worked the knocker vigorously on the front door for some minutes that I attracted the attention of Mrs. Huggins.

"Where's the nearest doctor?" I asked.

"Aren't you feeling well, sir? Would you like me to get you a drop of something?"

"No, no, I'm all right. It's not for myself I want him."

"Well, now," said Mrs. Huggins, "which doctor would you be wanting, sir? Dr. Armstrong or Dr. Smith? Dr. Smith

we always has; he eased my John's rheumatism something
wonderful, and I'd always tell any one—"

"I don't care which," I interrupted, "but whichever's
nearest."

"And who might you be wanting him for, sir, if I may
ask, for one of 'em lives one way and one t'other, so it all
depends where you has to go like?"

"Oh, well, the fact is," I said in desperation, "there's
a car standing on Cheney's avenue, and a man in it who
is either dead, or seriously ill, and I want to get a doctor
immediately."

"Well, now, my gracious, just fancy that! I'm sure I
don't know what things are coming to. But there, I always
did say as them there motor-cars—I haven't no patience
with 'em, the dangerous things, nor I'm not likely to have,
seeing as how only last Wednesday week, when my Doris
was going over the way to Mr. Jones—that's the grocer,
sir—for a couple of pounds of sugar, and he hadn't no
change for some reason, and she come running back to get
it, and one of them there cars comes along caring for nobody, and blows its great horn just behind my girl's back,
and frightens her so she falls on the pavement and bruises
her knee, and heaven knows—"

At this juncture Forbes appeared. "Why, Kent, what's
the matter? Somebody drowning or dead, or what?"

"Why, yes," I answered, "something of the kind. But
what do you know about it?"

"Nothing at all. But a respectable person like yourself
doesn't run about before breakfast with a creel, but no
rod, unless the circumstances are unusual."

I looked at my empty hands, and remembered for the
first time that I had left my rod on the footboard of the
car—a circumstance which made me the more anxious to
get back with all possible speed. I told Forbes in a few
words what had happened.

"This is odd," said Forbes, "and interesting. If you have no objection I should like to come back with you. I shall have time enough to get back."

"I shall be glad to have your moral support," I assured him. "I have been inquiring where the doctor lives, but without success so far."

"I happen to know that," Forbes replied. "It is only two or three minutes' walk. Let us go immediately. Time may or may not be of importance, but we had better waste as little as we can. Still, you will hardly want your creel. You may as well leave it behind you."

2

The Curious Conduct of Horton Forbes

Forbes walked with a long stride, with which I found it a little difficult to keep up, being still rather out of breath with running; for although to my impatience it seemed like half-an-hour since I had entered the hotel, the church clock, as we came outside, showed me that, in fact, it was exactly five minutes; and in another two we were ringing the bell of a pleasant Georgian house, on the door of which was a brass plate with the simple inscription, "Dr. Armstrong."

In a few seconds an upstairs window was opened, and a head was thrust out. So far as I could see the face through the masses of lather, it appeared to belong to a young man, in a fine physical condition, and of a cheerful temperament.

"Anything urgent?" he called, suspending his razor over his right cheek.

"Yes," said Forbes. "Man ill or dead in a car in Cheney's avenue. Better come at once, if you can."

In three or four minutes the doctor joined us. He seemed to be full of health and energy, and showed no sign of annoyance at being swooped upon before he was dressed; nor did the prospect of examining a dead man before breakfast appear to affect his spirits in the slightest degree. "I have telephoned for an ambulance," he remarked, "and it will probably turn up pretty soon, but we may as well walk on in the meantime, if you care to." As we all set off together he added: "Which of you was it that found this man? Or were you both together?"

"I did," I said. "I was on my way to fish the stream at Cheney's place. Kent, my name is."

"So you," he said, turning to Forbes, who was on his other side, "have not seen him yet?"

"No," he answered. "That's why I'm coming along now. And allow me also to introduce myself. My name is Horton Forbes."

"Not by any chance the Horton Forbes who published a monograph on Phoenician Rites in the West Country?"

"I'm afraid so," said Forbes with a smile.

The doctor nodded appreciatively, but did not pursue the subject. "And what," he asked me, "made you think this man was dead? You are confident that he wasn't simply asleep, or fainting?"

"Well, really," I said, "I hardly know what it was that made me think him dead. I have had so little experience of these matters. Even now I don't feel sure, because I can't think of any one definite thing which made me suppose him to be dead, but his general appearance certainly made me think so."

"Quite so," he said. "Well, anyhow, we shall soon see."

I was beginning to have a most uncomfortable feeling that possibly I was bringing these people on a fool's errand, and that when we got to the place we should find that the car had gone and that there had never been anything more in it than a tired man coming home late and falling asleep over the wheel. In that case, I should indeed look foolish. The doctor interrupted my thoughts with a further question:

"What was this man like? Tall, short, fat, thin, or how?"

"He was an elderly man," I answered. "With white hair over his ears. I should say he was slight, and not very tall. He had an intellectual face—rather delicate features, and I took him to be possibly a scholar, certainly a gentleman."

"Was he wearing a black coat—jacket, I mean?"

"Now you mention it, I fancy he was. Yes, I feel almost sure he was; also, I believe, dark trousers, and a dark grey cap."

"It sounds," said Dr. Armstrong, "remarkably like Professor Cheney himself. If so, the case is probably a simple one. I have been expecting something of the kind."

"The Professor had some infirmity, then?" said Forbes, speaking for the first time for some minutes.

"Heart disease," answered Armstrong. "Complicated by fatty degeneration. Yes, for some time past this might have happened at any moment; and if it is the Professor, as I expect, we shall probably not have to look far for the cause of death, that is, if he is dead. But here, I think, is our ambulance, so we can save our guesses till we see."

The purr of a car behind us became distinct, and presently the ambulance drew up. Forbes and the doctor got inside, and I mounted the seat by the driver. In a minute we were at the entrance gates, and as we swept round the curve to the right, opening the straight stretch in front of us, I fear that I was relieved, rather than distressed, to see that the car at least was still there. I was further glad to see, as we stopped behind it, that my rod lay where I had left it, and that no sign was visible at first sight that any one had since been near the place.

The other two were out of the ambulance as soon as I was, and we approached the car together. Forbes went to the right of it, while the doctor and I went to the left. It was a two-seater, with one door, which the doctor opened and leaned through to examine the occupant, while I waited outside. After a couple of minutes he withdrew, and said to me and to the driver of the ambulance, who had come up meanwhile:

"Yes, it is Professor Cheney, and he is dead. Dead several hours. The first thing to do is to shift him outside, which may not be too easy."

"Did you say," called Forbes, from the other side of the car, "that he had been dead several hours? Are you sure of that?"

"Perfectly sure," he answered. "At least, for practical purposes, I should say four hours at least."

"You are confident he died not less than four hours ago?"

"Yes, yes, my dear sir, I just said so. Excuse my abruptness, but I've just knocked my head on this infernal screw. If you will help me from that side, Mr. Forbes, we'll attend to this. Once we get the poor old boy clear of the wheel, it's all right."

It was a difficult and gruesome business, and took some time. At length, however, the body was laid on a stretcher, and carried to the ambulance, where the doctor made an examination of it. While he was thus engaged, I turned to talk to Forbes; but found that he was sitting on a heap of stones by the side of the road, gazing with intense concentration at a large thistle that happened to be growing near by. He was clearly, but for some reason inexplicable to me, lost in profound thought. I saw that he was not inclined for conversation, and I was beginning to feel the need of breakfast myself. So I sat down on the next heap and lit a cigarette.

Presently the doctor reappeared, and Forbes came to life again.

"I can find no trace," said the doctor, "of anything inconsistent with the obvious explanation of his death. I can find no injury of any kind, and I think it's simply a case of failure of the heart."

"You would be prepared to certify death from heart disease, I suppose?" said Forbes.

"Certainly. As I said, I know his heart was wrong, and have been expecting this. I think, Kent, it would be as well, since you found him first, if you would come up to the house with me. Lady Cheney might wish to see you."

"Of course I will," I answered. "I ought at least to offer my condolences. I expect I shan't be long, Forbes, and I hope I shall be back before you leave."

Saying which, I took my former seat beside the driver, while Dr. Armstrong went inside with the body. As we bowled along at a moderate pace down the straight, slightly sloping road, I was free to notice the water I had originally meant to fish. On the left was a fair-sized lake, and the road on reaching it turned pretty sharply to the right over a humpy bridge, beneath which ran a stream, with a swift and broken current, winding away down the valley. Then the road went on in the direction taken at the bridge, uphill between old elm trees to the house, some half-mile further on.

The door was opened by a maidservant, and Dr. Armstrong asked for Lady Cheney.

"Her ladyship is not down yet," the girl answered. "But Miss Cheney is, if you would wish to see her."

"Very well," he said. "Perhaps that will be best after all."

We followed the servant into a large room with windows looking towards the lake, walls lined with books, deep red leather chairs, and an old-fashioned, open fireplace—doubtless the Professor's study, and very pleasant and comfortable it looked. I was studying the backs of some formidable scientific treatises when the door opened, and a charming girl came into the room. She greeted the doctor, and looked inquiringly at me. He, however, began at once.

"I am exceedingly sorry, Miss Cheney, to be the bearer of very sad news for you. It was your father's heart. You have been fearing it, I know, but I am afraid that doesn't make it easier when it comes."

It was very painful for all of us. I need not say more of it than that she bore it very bravely, and I left the house half-feeling that I, as well as she, had been bereaved, although indeed I had never seen Professor Cheney alive. The body was taken into the house, and I left the doctor there, while I walked on as far as the bridge. I leaned over it, and watched the clear lake water tumble foaming into the stream beneath, until I was roused from a reverie by the sound of the ambulance coming back. It stopped, and I got in.

"Well, it's a horrid business, Kent," said Armstrong. "This is a part of my work which I detest."

I made some ordinary reply, and relapsed into silence, being occupied with my own thoughts, from which I was again roused by hearing the doctor call: "What, not gone yet?"

Looking out, I saw that we had just passed the car, which was still standing where we left it; and there, with his head under the open bonnet, was Horton Forbes.

We stopped, and I got out. The doctor, being due at his surgery at nine, could afford no more time, so went on.

"Good heavens, Forbes!" I exclaimed. "I thought you were due away at nine? It's half-past eight now. Whatever are you doing?"

As far as I could see, he was adjusting the carburetor, which seemed to me a most extraordinary occupation in the circumstances.

"I wonder," he muttered. "Oh, but anyway, there was a moon."

Now I really knew nothing of this strange person, except that there seemed a certain mystery about him, and a certain charm of manner that had attracted me. Now I began to suspect him of being an amiable lunatic.

Presently, looking up, he blandly remarked:

"Oh, it's you, Kent. Yes, there were one or two things about this car that have interested me. I shall have to postpone my business at Abergavenny. I wonder whether you feel like a little stroll? Your rod is still here, by the way, and we might as well just have a look at the lake, what?"

"Hang it all, Forbes," I answered irritably. "I've seen the lake already. Breakfast seems to me the word at present."

"It's only a step," he suggested, with an ingratiating smile—I am bound to admit it was ingratiating—and anyhow I went. When I got there, I resumed my position on the bridge, but there was no chance for sentiment this time. For Forbes calmly got out my rod and put it together; next, after fumbling in his pockets, attached something to the line; then cast, and immediately withdrew the line again, not by winding it on the reel, but by carefully lifting the rod. He passed the line through his fingers, and measured some of it with a tape measure. I could see no sense in these proceedings, and when, having disjointed the rod, he suggested that we should go back and have breakfast, I was genuinely surprised to hear him say anything so sensible.

3
BRADSHAW AND BREAKFAST

An appetising smell of fried bacon greeted us as we entered the portals of the "White Hart," and we were soon enjoying as welcome a meal as I had tasted for a long time. But before he sat down, Forbes opened a suit-case, from which he took a Bradshaw. He would take a mouthful of eggs and bacon, lay down his knife and fork, and ruminatively contemplate first one page and then another, turn over to another table and repeat the process. When at last he spoke I had forgotten his very existence, being lost in thoughts of Miss Cheney.

"We seem to have been thrown together in a rather curious way," he remarked. "And I was wondering if by any chance you would be disposed to help me in some inquiries that I think of making? I can promise you that they will be not uninteresting, and might even provide more excitement than fishing; and some quite as improbable stories."

"It depends," I answered, "on what sort of inquiries you mean, and what you want me to do. Also where you want me to do it." For I had no intention of allowing myself to be dragged away from Cheney Park without very good reason.

"That," he replied, "I can hardly say, at present, with absolute definiteness, but I can give you a rough idea. Let me first of all tell you something about myself, unless you feel that you already know all that is necessary?"

"Certainly I can't say that," I said. "Your actions have bewildered me more than once, and I shall be glad to hear whatever you like to tell me. Besides, we only met last night."

Forbes smiled and lit a long Turkish cigarette.

"After I took my schools at Oxford," he began, "it was my intention to become a doctor. But I found that though the theoretical part of the work interested me enormously, and I became fairly competent in that respect, the practical part was distasteful, and I neglected it. My father, who was something of a martinet, insisted on my immediately abandoning this trifling, as he called it, and going into the jute business. Jute, Kent," he continued, gazing at me with a quaintly sorrowful expression, "is, I regret to say, one of those substances which appear to me to be totally without fascination. I took no interest in it. Even when on Monday I had bought enormous quantities of jute, I felt no happier than I did on Tuesday, when I had sold, and probably sold short, still more enormous quantities. At this juncture an uncle of mine died—an uncle I had never seen—and left me his entire fortune. He had made it in jute."

Here Forbes paused, as though the last word about everything had been said, and looked up as if expecting the fall of the curtain.

"Go on," I said. "What then?"

"Then, Kent, I disentangled myself from jute, and followed my own inclinations. My inclinations lead me invariably to interest myself in anything uncommon or incredible. I like to be able to appreciate the queer feelings, and to see from the strange points of view, that are to be found either among exceptional people of one's own race, or else in civilisations very different from our own. For this reason I spent some years travelling in countries such as Persia

and Siam, which still remain comparatively free from
modernity; but I find now that one may easily come across
people quite as strange, and occurrences quite as stimulating, here at home. Does anything I have said so far make
you feel inclined to interrupt your fishing to some extent,
and to become, as it were, a fisher of men for a time?"

Attracted though I was by the proposal of adventure, I
thought it best to answer cautiously.

"I rather like the idea," I said. "But, so far, I have
no notion what it is all about; nor can I see how I could
possibly be of any use to you. My work doesn't help me
much to qualify as a dealer in mysteries. I am a master at
Lowchester."

"I had inferred so," said he. "But for that very reason
I think you would fit in very well. I don't want any one
who either is, or looks, mysterious. I want some one who
is not likely to be thought so, but some one also who has a
sufficiency of commonsense, decision and courage. If you
consented, I should be glad."

This was somewhat flattering. I began to feel more disposed to accept the unusual invitation.

"But still," I urged, "you have given me no notion what
all this is about."

"I have to be reticent," he replied, "until I know how
we stand. But I will say this. There have lately been a
number of unaccountable disappearances, and the police
have not succeeded in accounting for them. When I said
I was an insurance agent, I spoke in a metaphorical sense,
but at any rate, one or two people have consulted me, in
great distress, about the disappearance of relatives, and
quite recently I seemed to get traces leading to this part of
the country. The same is true of a case with which I personally was unconnected, but which created more stir than
all the rest of them. I mean the case of Caspian Orme. You
probably recall the name. He was an American millionaire,

who came to England after many years in China, where he
accumulated a large fortune. I saw him about London once
or twice. He was a man with a lean, lined, yellow face, a
hooked nose with wide nostrils, a stoop, which brought
his head down on his shoulders, and which, together with
his dead-black hair and piercing eyes, won him the unkind
name of 'the Vulture from Shanghai.'" Forbes opened his
suit-case again, and produced a pile of newspaper cuttings. "That is all I know of him personally," he continued. "And his case would have had no special interest for
me but for the fact which you will see at the end of this
newspaper paragraph."

This is what I read:

> Considerable excitement has been caused in
> social and financial circles by the disappear-
> ance of the American millionaire, Mr. Caspi-
> an Orme, who recently came to this country.
> He owns a fine property in Surrey, where he
> has lived alone, except for his staff of Chinese
> servants, who have been with him many years.
> He went out for a walk last Sunday morning,
> but failed to return, and has not since been
> heard of.
>
> It now transpires that he had recently
> placed almost the whole of his immense for-
> tune in bearer securities, and that these also
> have vanished. It is feared that he has become
> the victim of foul play, of which the motive
> was robbery on a gigantic scale.
>
> Additional evidence pointing in this direc-
> tion came into the hands of the police yester-
> day, when an ebony walking-stick, belonging
> to Mr. Orme, was discovered in the corner of
> a deserted barn in Monmouthshire. The clue

is being followed up, and it is hoped that
fresh light will soon be shed on the mystery.

"No light has been shed, however," Forbes said, as he
replaced the cutting in its place. "I feel sure that somewhere in this part of the country is to be found the source
of these crimes; but the traces are faint and doubtful, and
so far have brought me to no definite goal. Disappearances
like this are, of course, constantly happening; but not only
have these been more numerous than usual, but, according to my feeling, they are somehow connected with each
other. Whatever the mystery may be, it is one that I should
greatly like to elucidate."

"Well, Forbes," I said at last, "I'll come with you; that
is, of course, as far as my time and means allow."

"I am delighted to hear you say so," he responded; "but
I certainly mustn't let you commit yourself like this without pointing out that our quest is one likely to be attended by a certain amount of risk. How much risk, or of what
nature, I cannot say, being still very much in the dark. But
the person or persons behind these things have shown considerable cunning, and it is not to be supposed that they
are over-scrupulous, or would hesitate to deal savagely
with intruders. And it may be a wild-goose chase at that."

I am not one of those strange people who love danger
for its own sake, and positively struggle to get themselves
into a tight corner; but I was not to be deterred from what
promised to be an interesting adventure by the possibility
of some vague risk; and I said so with decision.

"Then very many thanks, Kent," said Forbes. "I shall
be glad to have you with me, and we will regard it as set-
tled. I suppose you have no business which requires your
attention for a week or two?"

"No; I am perfectly free for a month. I had meant to go
home after spending a week here, but it is not in any way

essential. I hope, however, that we shall not have to leave here immediately? I—well, I should like to attend the Professor's funeral, you know."

"I think that will be all right," he answered. "I don't anticipate at present that we shall have to move our base, though I can't promise. By the way did you happen to inquire where the Professor had been yesterday?"

"No, it never occurred to me to ask, I'm afraid."

"It's of no consequence. Perhaps the doctor may know. We might ask him as we go out. If you feel equal to walking to Knighton, I was proposing to catch the 11.42 there.

"Certainly, I should like the walk. But why Knighton? Isn't Bucknell nearer from here?"

"True, it is somewhat nearer, but no poet, so far as I know, has considered it worthy of his muse, and I therefore suggest, respectfully but firmly, that Knighton should be our Mecca this morning. Do we see eye to eye?"

A little later we again set out, and as we walked to the doctor's house, it occurred to me to ask my companion what he had found to interest him in the Professor's car that morning.

"It struck me as being unusual in several ways," he replied. "But tell me, what did you yourself notice about it?"

"Nothing exceptional. It was an Ensign two-seater, in nice condition, evidently carefully kept—mileage 8,000 odd, upholstered in brown, balloon tyres—"

Forbes waved a long, artistic hand at me, as if giving me an episcopal benediction, and said:

"The make of the car being fortunately known, I think we may take the specification as read. You didn't, I suppose, touch anything inside?"

"No," I replied briefly. My efforts as a Sherlock Holmes had fallen a bit flat.

"Well," he resumed, "the points which struck me were five. First, the steering was extremely stiff. It was barely possible to deflect the wheels. Secondly, the lowest gear was engaged. Thirdly, the radiator was, only just perceptibly, warm. Forth, the lights were switched off. Fifth, the ignition was switched on. What do you make of that?"

I made nothing of it at all. It seemed to me a quite commonplace state of affairs and to indicate nothing whatever. I could only say:

"I see nothing remarkable about it. What do you make of it?"

"Well, the explanation will take a little time, and can wait till we get into the train. Meanwhile, here we are."

We rang the bell, and Forbes sent the doctor a message that he was sorry to interrupt him at a busy time, but would be grateful if he could spare a couple of minutes. When he appeared shortly afterwards, disclosing, as he opened the door, a queue of patients waiting, he seemed rather less full of bonhomie than on our previous meeting.

"My friend here," began Forbes, "is getting bothered about whether he will have to attend an inquest, and as we were passing, we ventured to call in and ask."

This was news to me. The thought of an inquest had never entered my head. The doctor merely replied that if an inquest were held, I should no doubt be required, but at present he had no information. Nor was he able to answer an inquiry about the funeral arrangements, in which Forbes seemed to take great interest. Failing to elicit any information, Forbes thanked him, and as he turned to go said casually:

"Where had the Professor been yesterday?"

"No one knows, apparently," Armstrong answered. "It seems that Lady Cheney and her daughter were out. He had tea as usual at 4.30, and shortly afterwards one of the maids thought she heard the car drive off, but no one saw him go. Probably he went to see some friend, in which case we shall hear as soon as news of his death becomes known."

"Didn't Lady Cheney feel any anxiety about him?" asked Forbes.

"I gathered," said Armstrong, "that it was not unusual for the Professor to go off, and not appear for dinner; and even though he was not back when she went to bed, she did not think it of serious importance."

As we resumed our journey I remarked to Forbes: "You didn't manage to get much news in that quarter."

"On the contrary, I think I got information of the highest importance. And as I may want a little time to spare in Knighton, I propose that we charter the hotel 'bus. It is rather an ancient vehicle, recalling the old diligence that Tartarin found in Algeria, but it may take us there quicker than our feet."

While awaiting the arrival of the 'bus I remarked to Forbes: "You are being very mysterious. Why don't you tell me where we are going, and what we are after?"

"We will begin," he replied, "by looking round for the murderer of Professor Cheney."

4

THE FIFTH FACT

I smiled faintly, trying to conceal my astonishment. But my manner betrayed me.

"Think it over," said Forbes. "Ah, here comes our 'bus."

I thought it over. At first I could see no reason to doubt the doctor's verdict—death from heart failure. But Forbes held a different opinion, and Forbes was clearly no fool. I recalled his points about the car. The ignition was on, and the engine therefore ready to run; but evidently it was not running at the time when the car came to a standstill. Therefore, the car must have been stopped, and the engine also. Was the engine stopped by being switched off? Very likely; but if so it was switched on again. Alternatively, it might have been stopped by letting the clutch in too suddenly—but perhaps that was not very probable, if the car was in low gear—or by failure of some kind. Then again, did this stoppage occur before the Professor's death or after it? Probably before, surely, for it was unlikely that the car could travel safely, as it apparently did, with only a dead man inside it. And I remembered the road quite distinctly enough to see that it could certainly not have rounded the bend some quarter of a mile back under its own guidance. I concluded, therefore, that the stoppage occurred before the death; and I thought it probable that, feeling ill, the Professor had stopped the car, and switched off the engine, while he rested to recover; and that then, feeling a little better, or in anxiety to get home, for he was little more than half a mile away, he had switched on again, got into gear, and was just leaning forward to press the self-starter, when he was overtaken by the fatal seizure from which he died. This seemed to me a perfectly feasible explanation; and by the time I reached it, for it took no little time to perceive the significance of the facts, I felt I had a theory that would hold water. I was on the point of telling Forbes—who in the meantime was placidly regarding the landscape—the conclusion I had come to, when I remembered that I had only considered two of his points—the two which had been, for some reason, uppermost in my mind. What were the others? The steering, he had said, was unusually stiff. I reflected about that for some time; but beyond the fact, which I saw immediately, that it made completely impossible the idea of the car having come round the bend without guidance—not a great gain, for it seemed impossible in any case—I could see no significance in the fact whatever.

Then there remained—what else was it? Yes, the lights were switched off. The doctor had said the Professor had been dead for some hours at 7 a.m., and it must therefore have been dark when he was on his way home. Why did he not use his lights? Well, who could say? Perhaps he turned them out—inadvertently—when he stopped the car? Or since there was a bright moon, the lights were confusing rather than helpful, and he turned them off when he reached his private drive. Or again—and this, I thought, was really rather brilliant—perhaps when he got a little way down the hill leading towards his lake, he ran into a fog—in which case he could see better without lights than with them? No, I felt certain nothing could be made of the lights; and I really felt very serious doubts whether Forbes had not come to a perfectly absurd conclusion. I could still see nothing that fitted in with the murder theory, still less suggested it. Was he not, in fact, taking me on a wild-goose chase? Apart from this, too, even supposing he had any ground for imagining that murder had been committed, what possible means could he conceivably have of knowing where the hypothetical murderer was to be found. What was all this business of going off to Knighton and catching the 11.42 to a destination not revealed? Was I being a consummate fool, in trusting Forbes like this on a mere acquaintanceship begun in this queer casual way? I began to think so. I could form no idea what his designs might be, but that this story of a murder was a cock-and-bull story seemed to be clearer every minute.

I was on the point of telling him that I considered this chase absurd, and that if he wished me to go on with it he must give me better reasons than he had yet done, when the 'bus came to a stop at our destination. I had been too absorbed in my thoughts to notice where we were, and any opportunity of taking Forbes to task was lost for the moment, for as soon as we alighted from our antique conveyance, he went off somewhere, telling me to meet him at the station in twenty minutes.

When at last we were seated in a first-class smoking compartment, which we fortunately kept to ourselves, my first feeling of irritation was replaced by curiosity to know how Forbes could justify himself; and as soon as I had got my pipe going, and he had lighted one of his long Turkish cigarettes, I opened the attack by saying:

"I have thought over your five interesting points, and they seem to me quite inconsistent with any idea of murder." And then I explained to him my theory of what had occurred.

To this he listened with flattering attentiveness, nodding his head several times, as if light were dawning at last, and I felt that I had convinced him. At the end he said:

"I think, Kent, that is quite sound reasoning—quite sound." But I was a little dashed when he continued: "I followed much the same course of thought myself this morning, while sitting on that heap of stones. But you say you have considered my five points—you have only actually mentioned four—just look at those daffodils! What a perfectly delicious sight. I don't wonder they made even Wordsworth break into poetry, do you? Yes, you seem not to have attached quite adequate importance to the radiator. However, I will console you by saying that if I could have got no further than those five facts, I should only have been justified in suspecting. I could not have been positive. Fortunately, I was able to see that those facts were not without significance, and to search for further material without loss of time."

That at least I was obliged to acknowledge. Whatever he had found, he had done it all in less time than I took to see any meaning in the facts he had given me.

"And what new clues did you find?" I said sarcastically. "Splashes of blood on the bonnet or a baby's toe tied to the driving mirror, or what?"

"Nothing quite as conclusive as that," said he, smiling. "But you shall see for yourself. And I ought perhaps to have mentioned—though it was not in itself a singular circumstance—that the hand throttle was open sufficiently to carry the car along at a moderate pace."

Here he produced, from a pocket-book, two small screwed-up bits of paper, and a jet key, and laid them on the seat at his side.

"This," he said, indicating one scrap of paper, "we will call Exhibit 1; this jet key we will call Exhibit 2; and this Exhibit 3. Now let me tell you the bearing of the facts as I saw it. My first discovery was the warmth of the radiator—and it was an accidental discovery, due to my habit of prying vaguely about. I inferred immediately that the

Professor must either have died within the last four hours at the outside, or that the engine continued running after he was dead. It was a pretty cold night, though there was not a great deal of wind, and as I ascertained that there was a full supply of water I should say the radiator could not have become nearly cold in less than two hours, and would certainly not remain warm more than four at the outside. Do you agree so far?"

"Yes," I answered. "I think that does seem pretty clear."

"The natural inference, therefore—in fact, the only inference possible, considering the fact that the car was in gear, that it could not have held the road round the bend after the Professor's death, and the engine, consequently, could not have run after his death—was, that he died from two to five hours before 6—*i.e.,* between 3 and 5 a.m.

"This was clearly a remarkable circumstance. What could bring him home at such an hour? I observed the speedometer, and found that it gave the length of the run at 63 miles—a distance which, if correct, could have been covered in two hours or less. From what I could see of the Professor, I inclined to think he had not died so lately, and just then Dr. Armstrong definitely gave the same opinion."

"Ah, yes!" I interrupted. "I remember now that you seemed struck with that."

"Quite so," he replied. "It showed that something had occurred of which there was no obvious explanation, and when an occurrence of that kind is associated with a corpse, some inquisitiveness may be pardoned. I took the liberty, while helping with the removal of the body, to explore the Professor's clothes. In the left upper pocket of his waistcoat, I found Exhibit 1, which I now produce.

"When unfolded, this proved to be a small piece of thin paper, of good quality, on which was typed:

2011325

Queen's Square

It did not enlighten me, but nevertheless it appeared suggestive. We can discuss it presently. I next considered what could be the explanation of the warmth of the radiator, supposing the Professor to have been dead more than four hours. Obviously, the most apparent one was that some one else had driven the car, with the body in it. This was not conclusive, for he might have died exactly at the four hours, assuming that to be the limit of time for the radiator on the one hand, and his condition, on the other; but such an exact timing seemed a somewhat improbable coincidence. On the other hand, no honest person would be likely to drive the dead Professor nearly home, and then abandon him and disappear.

"I sought, therefore, for further enlightenment. The fact that the lights were switched off, as I noted, while it would be extremely natural if a murderer were returning with his victim, would be a little odd if the Professor were driving home in the ordinary way—although explicable, no doubt, as you have said. The question why the car was in low gear puzzled me for some time, and I arrived first at a theory very like your own; only I supposed that the Professor had actually started the engine, and in a spasm of pain had suddenly released his pressure on the clutch, and the sudden weight stopped the engine. And there, my dear fellow, you were at a disadvantage in not having noticed, or connected, another fact with which you were, however, acquainted. It occurred to me to ask what would have happened supposing the jar of the clutch had not stopped the engine? And I immediately perceived that as the car had been running perfectly straight down the centre of the road for some quarter of a mile—which by the tracks I could see to have been the case—and it was then, by the way, that just over the brow of the hill, some two hundred yards behind the car, I picked up Exhibit 2—if it continued to run straight, it would inevitably end its career in the lake."

"By Jove, Forbes," I said. "That's a devilish suspicious circumstance, certainly. And I quite agree with you that it would; I remember thinking that it would be a dangerous corner for any one who didn't know the road."

"Yes," he continued, "and when, on investigation, I found that it was almost impossible to move the front wheels to either side, and when on further investigation, I found that there is a bank of granite blocks, on which tracks would be invisible, from the road to the lake, and that the lake on that point is over twelve feet deep, suspicion almost amounted to certainty."

"Ah! now I understand," I exclaimed, "your strange proceedings with my rod. I couldn't make out what on earth you were up to at the time, but I begin to think I must be a most awful fool not to have been able to spot what you were after."

"Not being in possession of any of the necessary material," replied Forbes, "you were even worse off than the Israelites, who had to make bricks without straw. But in saying that on finding the water was over twelve feet deep my suspicion became certainty, I was anticipating somewhat the course of events; for I did not, as you remember, make that discovery until after your return from Cheney Park. But the mere fact that the car would have run into the lake, which, at the point we have reached, was all I actually knew, was enough to make the theory of a plot to murder the Professor, and abolish all trace of him, appear worthy of serious consideration. I therefore tried to work out what the plot could have been, and how it was carried out. As there was no wound, and no signs of violence or suffocation, the weapon used was evidently poison—some poison which left no visible marks. It might have been administered either in the car or out of it—a point about which I am unable to judge—but it was clear that, as soon as it had taken effect, the murderer, in order to accomplish his design of causing the car to disappear in the lake, would act as follows. He would have first to tamper with the steering, so that the car would not easily be deflected by any chance object or inequality in the road—though, as it happens, the road surface there is excellent—and he would probably do this as far away as possible from the objective, so as to test the setting of the wheels, and make sure that the car would travel in the exact direction aimed at. When satisfied of this, he would have to get into gear, and then he would have to arrange the body at the wheel—"

"Why," I interrupted, "need he do so? When the car disappeared, it would hardly matter whether it were at the wheel or not?"

"I fancy," he replied, "that our friend was taking no more chances than he could help. There was a faint possibility of some one seeing the car on its way to the bridge, and a possible chance that such a person might notice that no one was driving it. Further, if it should be discovered in the lake, and the Professor were found at the wheel, it would be less likely to arouse suspicion than if he were elsewhere. At any rate, I was obliged to assume that he had acted as I have said."

"And why," I said, "need he have engaged the gear, before arranging the body?"

"Really, Kent," he answered, smiling, "you are as bad as jury and counsel all rolled together. I think he would probably do so, because the gear lever being on the right-hand side it would not be easily accessible when the body was in position."

"Oh! of course, that is so. My question was unnecessary. Please go on with your admirable exposition, and I'll try not to interrupt again."

"It would be necessary," he went on, "to put out the clutch, which he could do by hand, and to start the engine; next, to open the throttle—if, as is perhaps more probable, he had not already done that while testing the set of the steering—and then gradually to let the clutch in, and as the car gathered way, to jump off and shut the door. So far this seemed feasible enough. It fitted in with the warmth of the radiator, with the absence of lights, and with the use of the low gear; for whereas, on what I may call your theory, the use of that gear could only be explained by the coincidence that he died in the moment of starting from a standstill—on this theory it was inevitable; for if the murderer had started in second, or top, which, as there was a gentle downward slope, might have been possible, it would have been difficult to get a smooth start, and the car would have gathered way too fast to make jumping off easy. It would also have been less likely to keep a perfectly straight course.

"But then I was confronted by a very serious obstacle. How could it possibly happen, firstly, that the car did not, in fact, reach the lake? And secondly, why on earth did the murderer go away before making certain that it had done so? For the theory involved the situation that he had, for some time of unknown duration, driven a car containing a man for whose death he was responsible; and even the most hardened ruffian will hardly drive about through the night over lonely roads, with a corpse, under the shadow, as it were, of the gallows, and yet take such a casual and happy-go-lucky view of the situation as calmly to leave his work unfinished, and the evidence of his crime at the mercy of any one with enough perspicacity to see it.

"These two questions at first seemed so unanswerable that I was tempted to abandon the murder theory altogether;

but in thinking over the first question, why the car never reached its destination, I saw that the murder theory would be confirmed, if there were some defect in the mechanism which caused the car, after travelling for some way apparently quite as it should, to come to a stop. It would explain why the ignition was on, and the car in gear and yet not moving, and would make the murderer's conduct in disappearing less inexplicable.

"I decided, therefore, to begin with the carburetor, and here I had better fortune than I had any right to expect."

At this point I repressed the interruption which I was going to make. But with what extraordinary quickness must he have arrived at these conclusions! For he had re-assembled the carburetor by the time I saw him at it, and I could not have been away altogether more than half-an-hour.

"And here," he went on, unfolding the other scrap of paper, "we put in Exhibit 3. Look at it for yourself. You will no doubt easily recognise what it is."

He handed me the flattened-out paper, on which was lying a very small piece of metal, which seemed to be steel, about one-sixteenth of an inch long, about the thickness of a medium-sized needle, but hollow and slightly tapering. I could think of no part of a car's mechanism from which it could have come, nor could I form any idea of the nature of the fragment. While I was speculating about this he continued:

"I found that wedged in the end of the main jet, and, of course, it was enough to account for the stoppage, by the fact that it cut off the petrol almost entirely. What was not so plain was how it got there. It is too big to pass through the mesh of the filter, and the most likely explanation was that the instrument from which it came had been used to clean the jet, or lift the float, and that the tip had been broken off in the operation; and this operation had almost certainly been performed at, or near, the spot where I found the jet key—our second exhibit. Probably, the operator, having had carburetor trouble, had taken out the jets and cleaned the carburetor, and after replacing the jets had laid the key on the running board while he finished his work, and had then overlooked it. When the car started, it fell in the road—fortunately for us. He would now suppose that the trouble was over—but as often happens, the carburetor was one too many for him—and so perhaps he was more prone to take for granted that the car, once started, would continue to go. But it was the worst piece of work he ever did, for it made the murder hypothesis almost indubitable."

"But why?" I said. "What is this thing?"

"I supposed you had discovered that," said Forbes. "It is the tip of a hypodermic needle."

5

WILMER DEEPING

I had barely time to assimilate this astonishing fact before
the train began to draw up at a wayside station, which was
plainly our destination; for, hastily repacking our "exhib-
its" in his case, Forbes opened the door, and sprang out
with an eager alacrity quite different from his usual rather
nonchalant manner.

I soon followed, and we found ourselves on a neat little
platform, with the name WILMER DEEPING picked out
in stones on the bank, amid a profusion of primroses and
neatly kept flower-beds. Only one official—a porter—was
in evidence; and striding up to him Forbes enquired, as he
gave up our tickets, what passengers arrived on the 5.35
that morning.

"Can't say," said the man briefly. "Warn't on duty."

However, on Forbes explaining genially that he would
consider the information good value at half-a-crown, the
man summoned a small boy, who was hanging about outside the station, and told him to "ask Bill what passengers
come on the 5.35, and look sharp about it."

In a very few minutes the boy was back with the information that no passengers had come. "But," he added
hopefully, "there was a powerful lot of milk-cans."

This, however, appeared poor consolation to my friend,
for his look of disappointment was almost ludicrous. He

stood with his hands folded behind him, his head bent down over the comparatively microscopic urchin, on his face an expression of pained deprecation like that of an early Christian martyr. I nearly laughed aloud. Nor did the boy know what to make of it, and when Forbes sadly presented him with sixpence he incontinently fled.

My disgruntled friend remained gazing at the spot where the boy had been, without seeming to notice the difference; and then suddenly raised his head and emitted a chuckle so infectious that my pent-up amusement could no longer be restrained. We stood and laughed at each other whole-heartedly for some time. Our friend the porter seemed to accept it as being now established that we were both mad, and disappeared.

Forbes grasped my arm, and as our merriment subsided, said: "Of course, Kent, what a fool I was! We were not likely to hear of him by asking the porter. Let us come this way." And so saying, he started off along the line by which our train had just come in.

"Are you aware, my good person," I said, "that we are trespassing on the property of the railway, and liable to be flung into a dungeon and robbed of forty shillings?"

"I am," he said. "But what say the Sacred Writings? 'He that wishes to escape on a raft from a deserted island should not forbear to lash the timbers in order to save rope.' If need be, we will pay the forty shillings. But ah! what have we here?"

We had returned about a hundred and fifty yards from the station, which was almost hidden round a bend of the line. On our right was a field of longish grass, separated from the railway by a wire fence five-and-a-half feet high, and lying at a slightly lower level. Through the grass was plainly visible a recently made track; and as we went to examine it, we saw half-way between two posts muddy marks on the three lower wires, which were set somewhat closer together than the upper ones; marks apparently made by some person who had climbed over.

Forbes, already on the other side, suddenly called to me.

"Kent, come here quickly. Look at this."

Almost before he had finished speaking, I had joined him.

"What is it?" I asked. For I could see nothing of much interest, except that the grass was flattened out in one place as though by a fall.

"I merely called you to pop over here," he said, "to see how you would do it; and I may say you did it remarkably neatly."

With an air of offended dignity I followed behind him as he pursued the track, walking alongside it in a curious limping manner. It was easy enough to follow, for the wet grass had kept the impression, though of course no foot-marks were visible. It led us diagonally across a corner of the field, through a thin place in the hedge, and along the left hedge of another grass field, which sloped gently upwards. Then it swung suddenly to the right and joined a cinder path, leading in one direction to the station, and in the other to a stile. And there we lost it.

"So," I said, as we halted on the path, "whoever may be this will-o'-the-wisp that we are chasing—and I expect he is some boy looking for birds' nests—we have now lost him for good and all. There is nothing whatever to tell us where he is gone, or anything at all about him, and it looks like taking the next train back."

"Beyond the obvious facts," replied Forbes, apparently slightly piqued, "that he is a bulky but fairly active man, about five foot eleven in height, who has damaged his left leg, and is well acquainted with this place, I must admit our information is defective. But we may also conjecture, I think, that he was in a hurry and that he did not court observation."

Having thus put me in my place, and seeing my bewildered look, he again laughed delightedly, and said with great good humour: "And now I suppose you want to know my reasons for these wild words?"

I agreed.

"Then tell me," he said, "how did you deal with that wire fence just now?"

"Why," said I, "I believe I got through it."

"You did," he answered, "and with remarkable speed. And so did I. So also would any ordinarily slim person, of ordinary activity. It is by far the easiest and quickest way. To climb over a wire fence of six strands is not so easy as it looks. When you reach the point of throwing your leg over to the other side, you have nothing firm to hold, and are very likely to topple over—a fate which our friend seems to have met. True, a mere boy might climb the fence for fun, but you will recollect that the top mudmark was only on the third strand. A boy would have had to go a strand higher.

"Further, some one had apparently alighted just there from a moving train; for there was a deep heel-mark in the soft ground just beyond the ballast, and another less deep, of the other heel. And it is reasonable to suppose that he was the same man as climbed the fence. Only a tolerably active man, however, can jump from a moving train."

During this discourse we had been walking along the cinder path towards the stile, and now we crossed it and emerged into a road, on the opposite side of which, about forty yards to our right, was a gate inscribed *The Laurels. Tradesmen's Entrance*. It was apparently a fair-sized place, but we could see other houses at some distance down the road. The inference however was, prima facie, that if our bulky friend had been making for a house, this was probably the one.

"It's the merest speculation, of course," said Forbes. "But I think it will be worth finding out who lives there. We have very little to go on, but we seem to have come right till now, unless those tracks from the railway are merely accidental in spite of my expectation that I should find them. In that case I should be quite at a loss. I wonder if there are any house agents in the village? If so, our best move might be to go to them."

We passed The Laurels—the house itself was not visible from the road—and reached the village, where we eventually found, near the station, an estate agent's office, and went inside. We were received by a clerk, to whom Forbes spun the yarn that we had been rather attracted by the situation of The Laurels, and should like to know if it were to let. The clerk replied that the owner, a Mrs. Brook-Sutton, was anxious to sell the property, but that in the meanwhile she had let it to the present tenant on a six months' agreement, which would expire at midsummer.

"And who, may I ask, is the tenant?" said Forbes. "Would he object to our looking over the house?"

"I shouldn't think so," was the answer. "He is the Rev. Fielding Shortditch. We can give you an order to view, if you think of buying a property."

This certainly appeared discouraging. A clergyman was unlikely to be jumping out of trains, and climbing wire fences, at 5.30 in the morning.

"I suppose," Forbes went on, apparently quite placid, "he will be the vicar here?"

"Oh! no," the clerk answered. "Mr. Griffiths White is our vicar. No, this gentleman, Mr. Shortditch, is, I believe, a missionary home for his health."

"I seem to remember a Shortditch," said my friend, unblushingly. "I wonder if this is by any chance the same? It's an uncommon name. Now the man I mean was a bulky person, slightly shorter than myself, and I believe he used to limp a bit. Is this gentleman anything like that?"

"Well," the clerk replied, "the description fits him well enough, except for the limp. I have never noticed his limping, but we don't see much of him here. Keeps himself to himself, I gather."

"Still, I shouldn't wonder if he's my man," Forbes answered, "and we will call and see. If you can give us an order to view, I shall be glad to look over the property."

This was soon arranged, and we left the office.

But as it was by this time getting on for two o'clock, we decided to have lunch before pursuing our quarry, and it was about an hour later that we found ourselves at the front gate of The Laurels, which was in the road at right angles to that into which the side gate opened.

The door was opened by a little old woman in black, who looked at us rather timidly out of bright eyes, like a blackbird examining a worm.

Forbes showed our order to view, and asked whether Mr. Fielding Shortditch would kindly allow us to take a look round.

"Mr. Shortish is out, sir," she answered. "Nor he didn't leave no word when he would be back, and I'd rather you'd call again, sir, if it's not troubling you, for Mr. Shortish is a terrible particular gentleman, and I don't know what he'd say to it."

"I am very sorry," interposed Forbes, "but unfortunately we have come some distance, and have only a short time to spare; and we shall both be very grateful if you will just let us have a look round. It is my friend, here, Mr. Kent, who is interested in the house. So I will explain to Mr. Shortditch, if he should come in, if you will put me somewhere where I can wait for him. I am sure he will raise no objection."

"Well, you see, sir, it isn't as if I knew you," said the old lady, rather tremulously. "And I don't know whether

I'm doing right, I'm sure. But come this way, sir. This is Mr. Shortish's room, and you can see him come up the path if he comes in."

"I have an idea, you know," said Forbes, "that I once met Mr. Shortditch somewhere abroad. Isn't he rather stout and tall—a little shorter than I am?"

"Yes, sir, and he has been abroad too, though I don't know where, I'm sure, for I never can remember the foreign names. He was a missioner though, in Howareye or some such place, and he had to come back for his health, that I do know. But still, he don't rest now he is here, for he's always about one place or another."

"So I gathered in the village. My informant, in fact, thought he went away yesterday evening."

"Oh, no, he didn't, sir, not yesterday, for I put him his supper yesterday at half-past seven, the same as usual, and called him this morning too, and he didn't go out at all yesterday, not even in the afternoon."

Forbes and I exchanged glances.

It certainly was pretty evident that we had drawn a blank. However, he still persisted, encouraged by the fact that the old woman was forgetting her fear of us and was growing more ready to enjoy a little gossip.

"Mr. Shortditch will be an early riser, I daresay?" said Forbes. "People accustomed to other climates often are. I expect you have to be about pretty early in the morning, eh?"

"I comes in every morning at half-past six, sir," she said. "And it isn't often I'm late either. I don't hold with coming down any time you please, and as you please, like these girls nowadays, and Mr. Shortish would say the same. Then I lights the kitchen fire, and hots the water, and I calls Mr. Shortish up at half-past seven, all except Sundays when it's half-past eight."

"And you called him at half-past seven this morning, I suppose?"

"Yes, sir, and fast asleep he was too. I couldn't hardly wake him when I went in with his hot water, though he's not a heavy sleeper as a rule."

"It's a quiet life for him here, though. He'd have been accustomed to more coming and going, I expect. But he has friends in the neighbourhood, perhaps?"

"Not as I knows of, sir. Gentlemen do come and see him, now and again, as you might say, but there's not been any this month or more."

"Really. Well, it's a quiet life, but every man to his own likings. And what time do you leave him in the evening?"

"When I've put his supper on, sir, at half-past seven, is my time, and I'm often glad to reach it."

"Ah, well, Kent," said Forbes, turning to me, "you mustn't stand gossiping. Don't be too long over your investigations." And as the housekeeper went out of the door to show the way, he whispered: "Notice everything, but be quick. If possible I should like to get out before he comes back. I will look around here."

6

The Shyness of Fielding Shortditch

It was with very uncomfortable feelings that I followed the brisk little housekeeper up a flight of thickly-carpeted stairs. I was, it seemed to me, intruding wrongfully and deceitfully into this fellow's privacy. I could not seriously entertain the supposition that the occupant of this house had committed murder some twelve hours earlier; and my role as prospective house purchaser was not one that came naturally to me, for the whole of my resources did not amount to a thousand pounds.

On reaching the landing, which was without furniture and covered by linoleum, we turned to the right down a bare passage. It seemed endless, and took unexpected turns at right angles, as if it were trying to escape pursuit. This was the more unreasonable, as the house was quite modern, built, I supposed, about 1890, solidly but without taste. We looked into room after room, all unfurnished and featureless, except for dirty spiders' webs hanging from corners, bits of plaster that had peeled from ceilings, or designs in mildew on the wall-papers. Everywhere the dead air had the cold fustiness of a disused house; the place was as cheerless as a tomb. There was plainly nothing of interest to be seen in that quarter, and I proposed that we should glance into the rooms in the other wing.

One of these was rather poorly furnished as a spare
bedroom, but the bed was unmade, and there was nothing
to attract attention. Opposite was "Mr. Shortish's bedroom," as the housekeeper informed me, and she was for
passing it over, but I prevailed upon her to let me have a
look inside—so far as I could get it through a half-opened
door. There seemed, however, nothing remarkable. I noticed that the furniture was modern and quite undistinc-
tive, though excellent of its kind; the bed linen good; the
wall-paper somewhat flamboyant and quite new. Beside
the ordinary furniture, there was a large cabin trunk with
several old labels, a medicine chest in an angle of the wall,
and some illustrated papers—American apparently—in a
paper-stand near the head of the bed. Among the toilet
articles I noticed a tin of dental plate powder.

Relieved to have finished my uncongenial task, I was
quickly downstairs, and after a perfunctory glance round
the lower regions, returned to the room where we had left
Forbes.

Instead of finding him, as I had expected, pacing about
impatiently, agog to be gone, I saw him sitting, or rather
reclining at full length in an easy chair facing the window,
with his hands in his pockets and his eyes half closed. He
took no notice of my entrance, and I said pretty sharply:

"Come on, for the Lord's sake, and let's get out of this.
I couldn't take the house at a gift, and there's nothing at
all to see."

He opened his eyes, but made no move. On the contrary, he answered quietly:

"I fear, my dear Kent, that the fat is, to a certain
extent, in the fire. Your friend Horton has, I am sorry to
say, let you down. About five minutes ago, I was standing
by the writing-desk over there by the window, admiring its
amazing neatness—even the blotting-paper is unsullied—
when I saw a person pass the gate wearing a dark hat, a

high clerical collar, and a dark overcoat. He was looking into the house, and must have seen me at the window. At first I thought he was coming in—taking it for granted that he was our man—but instead of that he passed on behind the shrubbery. I must say that his general appearance did not appeal to me. 'Gross' would describe him perhaps more aptly than 'bulky,' and his face seemed to me unprepossessing—a large pale face, with small eyes, and an expression, as I fancied, of slinking hostility. He passed on, and nothing happened, until just as I had replaced an interesting chess problem which I have photographed as a curiosity"—here Forbes produced from his pocket a small but exquisitely made camera—"in that drawer, the second on the left, I looked up and was in time to notice a face move from an opening in the shrubs—and I have little doubt that it was our slinking friend. Fortunately, he could not have seen what I was actually doing, but he is clearly either incredibly shy or strangely suspicious, and I think our only course now is to wait a few minutes and try to relieve him of his fears. If he thinks we are watching him it may hamper our inquiries."

It went much against the grain with me to meet the fellow, and I longed to escape the ordeal, but it was obvious that Forbes was right. So while we waited I told him the few things upstairs that had caught my notice.

He said the American papers and the medicine chest might possibly be suggestive, if we could examine them, which did not, however, seem feasible, and then he told me his own discoveries.

"You will have seen," he began, "that the tidiness of this room is positively ghastly. There are no papers lying about, no opened letters on the writing-table, no books out of place—nothing. What is still stranger, not a single drawer is locked, and none of the drawers contains anything but the dullest things—proceedings of missionary and other religious societies, tracts, catalogues of books, sermon paper, newspaper cuttings, and so forth—not enough to incriminate a mouse."

I looked round the room and nodded. It was more like a board room than a bachelor's den.

"That is," he went on, "at first sight. But as I went into things closely, some interesting facts began to emerge. I began with the books—not seeing anything else to begin with—and picked one or two out at random. They both proved to have been bought secondhand, at a certain book-seller in the Charing Cross Road. I selected another shelf. Every book in it was bought secondhand, as the penciled prices showed, and all from the same shop. And the assort-ment was a strange one. The great majority were religious books. There was, for instance, a Greek text of The Acts, with Blass's Latin notes; a commentary in German on the Epistle to the Ephesians; a Grammar of Sanskrit; and an Old Testament in Hebrew. Next to those was the sum-ma of St. Thomas Aquinas, among which two old volumes of *Punch,* in a somewhat similar binding had strangely become entangled. I judged that our clerical friend had bought his books *en masse*—or else we are to be confronted by a prodigy of learning who sees no incongruity between *Punch* and the lean Aquinas.

"Again, his missionary interests are extensive. Those neatly arranged reports concern the proceedings of societ-ies of every shade of opinion, from Catholic to the other extreme, and working in three Continents. Once more I inferred: 'A job lot.' And 'There is something in this more than natural,' I said to myself, 'if philosophy could find it out.' Again I turned my attention to the drawers. But I was not rewarded. I came across nothing whatever pos-sessing any human interest at all, except the chess problem that I've mentioned. An odd kind of problem that. I am bound to say that our search has yielded very little, but it confirms my very strong—"

"Pardon me, gentlemen, but may I ask what you are doing here?"

We both turned round, startled. The door had opened noiselessly, and framed in it was the devil we were talking of. How he got in without our hearing a sound through the open window, or opened the door without our being aware of it, I can't say; but I know that I took an immediate dislike to the man. I disliked his small pale eyes, and the whole aspect of him. He had on a dark mackintosh, unbuttoned, and he kept his hat on his head and his hands in his pockets as he stood and looked at us.

I caught a sign from Forbes that I was to do the talking, and said:

"We owe you an apology, sir, for intruding in this way; but the fact is, this house rather caught my fancy as we passed it, and the agents told us it was for sale, and gave us an order to view. Your housekeeper asked us to wait for your return, but as she could not say how long you would be, I prevailed upon her to show me over. My friend here, however, caught sight of you passing the house a few minutes ago, and so we decided to wait and make our apologies."

"None are needed, sir, none are needed—believe me. Most happy, I am sure. My name, as you are perhaps aware, is Fielding Short-ditch—pronounced Shortish, you know."

We introduced ourselves, and he continued:

"Now you are here, you must have a cup of tea with me. No," waving a fat white hand at us, "no, I insist. It is an event to see visitors in this lonely spot. Pardon me a moment while I remove my outer raiment. We will have tea in directly."

In a moment he padded in again, like a soft-footed elephant clothed in clerical pepper and salt.

"You are fortunate, young fellow," he said to me, "in being in a position to buy a property such as this. And yet I sometimes feel perhaps this inherited wealth may be a curse—may be a curse. At least I never regret for myself that I was never rich enough to be idle in my young days. I would give much if I could prevail upon you young men to come forward and help the great Cause. But I see you don't know what I am talking of. My work for years has lain in the mission field, and it has been blest—much blest—and I often think, Mr. Kent, what a fine enterprise it would be for a young fellow of means to undertake who would otherwise be idle."

"As it happens," I said pretty coldly, "I am not idle. I happen to be a master at Lowchester, so I fear I am not available."

"Indeed," he replied suavely. "Indeed. But you would have opportunities there also—there also. No doubt there are earnest young men among the masters, and the lads, dear fellows . . . but I mustn't weary you with my hobby. Lowchester is in Yorkshire, I think, or Lincolnshire is it? Rather a far cry from here. What attracts you to this remote spot?"

I saw that I had made a blunder. I could think of no reason which could induce a young public school master to take an enormous house two or three hundred miles from his school. But Forbes came magnificently to the rescue.

"My friend Kent," he said genially, "is an awful instance of vaulting ambition. Not contented with a nice soft job at a public school, he wants to set up a school of his own. I try to dissuade him, though of course these large houses, which can be had so cheap, are a temptation. But how do you get about from here? You keep a car, I expect?"

"Oh, dear, no! No, my means are not large, and such as they are I must put them to other uses. Do you take sugar? No, I have never learnt to drive."

"You depend upon the trains, then?" Forbes remarked mildly. "I always hate that. One invariably has to dash off in the middle of something very important. Like time and tide, they wait for no man."

"I do not find that an inconvenience," he answered, with a sidelong look at each of us from under his thick, sandy eyebrows. "I am punctual from long habit. A little more tea?"

"No, thanks," I answered. "What about getting on, Forbes? Speaking of trains . . ."

"You are not motoring then?" said our host. Again I felt I had made a mistake of tactics, for trains are few at Wilmer Deeping, and our destination would not be hard to discover.

"No," said Forbes, "we shall walk some of the way, and perhaps take the train later on, if we are short of time. We had better be moving or we shall miss it altogether."

We said good-bye, with relief, and started. We walked to the next station, six miles away, and just caught the last train. As it drew out of the station a powerful limousine drove up, and a man got out and went into the booking-office. It was almost dark, but we both thought that we recognised the figure of the Rev. Fielding Shortditch.

7

DR. ARMSTRONG IS SCEPTICAL

We were tired out when we reached home. But something had been achieved, for I was now as convinced as Forbes was that the death of Professor Cheney was due to that fat slug of a man at The Laurels. The theoretical argument had not brought entire conviction, for, like most of us, I am distrustful—absurdly, perhaps—of mere reasoning. But I found a more effective argument in the odious Shortditch himself, and his apparent pursuit of us. I was all for going to the police at once, but Forbes ridiculed the idea.

"Consider," he said, "I beg you, oh! enthusiastic but premature Kent, that we have not one single particle or spark of evidence to which the officials could attend. They would be even less moved than you were by the train of reasoning which led me to that house at Wilmer, and rightly so, for they have not tested it. It convinces me, because I formed an hypothesis on what seemed to me logical grounds, and on that hypothesis I predicted certain future events. These events occurred, and so produced conviction of the truth of my hypothesis. But what evidence can we produce to the police? No, my dear fellow, they would laugh at us. And, frankly, I am not anxious to call them in until we must. We shall have more chance of success if we keep things as quiet as we can, for I feel that this murder is part of something still more sinister. You remember

the strange disappearance last summer of that promising
young Norwegian scientist, who was said to have invented
a deadly ray of amazing power, and was over here to offer
it to the British Government? He vanished, and so did his
ray, no one knows where. And the equally curious case of
the millionaire, Caspian Orme, who, as I have told you,
walked out of his house at Haslemere one Sunday morning, and has never since been heard of? The Professor's
death is also strange, and I should be glad to learn more
about it before I call in the police. However, we must tell
Dr. Armstrong, though I am prepared for incredulity in
that quarter also."

Accordingly, after supper, we dropped in at the doctor's
house, and were cordially welcomed. He produced whisky and soda and cigars, and gave us a very comfortable
and friendly evening in his cosy smoking-room. But he
was sceptical, undisguisedly. The only part of the evidence
that affected him at all was the piece of hypodermic
needle, but the fact that it was in the carburetor appeared
to make him feel that it could have no connection with the
Professor's death.

"After all," he argued, "your theory that some fellow
hooked the float out with it is all very well, but it seems a
bit far-fetched, and I know all sorts of extraordinary things
get into carburetors—the Lord alone knows how, but they
do. Still, I'll certainly have another look for any signs of a
hypodermic injection. The inquest is to be to-morrow, and
I was prepared to say, as I told you, 'natural causes,' but of
course if there's any doubt we shall have to go a bit deeper.
Even now, however, I can't quite believe it. The funeral is
fixed for Thursday—three o'clock." We rose to go.

"We shall attend," said Forbes, "if at all possible. So
you don't think we have much chance of getting our reverend criminal arrested?"

"It strikes me," said Armstrong, "from what you say the housekeeper told you, that he has a pretty good alibi. Everything as usual the night before, no one to see him, no car, no trains, thirty miles to travel, and fast asleep in bed at half-past seven in the morning—it seems pretty sound. No, your evidence isn't strong enough, Forbes, though I won't say there mayn't be something in it. Well, goodnight."

"Good-night," we answered. "Keep all this quiet, won't you?"

And we went off to our repose, for which I, at least, was very ready.

Next morning when I came down—not quite so early this time—there was no sign of my friend; but I found a note on my plate saying that he was following a line of inquiry that might or might not lead to something, and suggested that I should "represent the firm" at the inquest and interment, if he were still absent.

I found the intervening time tedious and depressing. At the inquest I had to give evidence of finding the body, but it was already known, and excited no interest. There was a feeling of expectancy in the court, however, when Dr. Armstrong was called upon.

"Can you say," inquired the coroner, "what was the cause of death?"

"Yes," the doctor replied firmly, "the cause of death was cardiac syncope—failure of the heart—of which the immediate occasion appears to have been a hypodermic injection of morphine."

This caused something of a sensation.

"Is there, so far as you can tell," asked the coroner, "anything to show by whom, or when, this injection was administered?"

"No," was the reply, "except that it must have been given very shortly before death, which probably occurred from four to twelve hours before I saw the body—that is, between 7 p.m. and 3 a.m."

"Could the injection have been made by the deceased himself?"

"Quite easily," the doctor answered. "It might even, conceivably, have been made accidentally."

The coroner put no further questions, but, after a whispered conference with the police, adjourned the inquest for a week for further evidence.

The rest of the day I wandered disconsolately about, able to settle to nothing, and not at all in a holiday spirit. As soon as I turned my thoughts from Mary Cheney, I began to miss the stimulating presence of Horton Forbes, and so I oscillated from one to the other—with occasional reminiscences of Fielding Shortditch—in a very unhappy frame of mind.

The day of the funeral was even worse; for, added to the melancholy which such an occasion must always inspire, even when it is connected with no personal loss, I shared, more than might have been expected, the genuine and evident grief of the chief mourners. I had not before seen Lady Cheney, but I felt drawn towards her at once. Her clear-cut, kindly face, which still kept a youthful look and colour, was graced by white hair, and seemed to reveal, beneath her unaffected sorrow, the light of a spirit too steadfast and serene to fear the intervention of death.

Afterwards, she sent me word that she and her daughter would think it a kindness if I would drive back to the house with them. They were, not unnaturally, very troubled by the doctor's discovery.

"We had hoped," said Lady Cheney, "that Mr. Forbes might be here to-day—although, of course, there was no reason why he should be. Dr. Armstrong hinted that he might be able to tell us something, and we are so very anxious. My husband never doctored himself, and we feel sure he would not have given himself a dangerous drug, which he never used; and then, if it was accidental, it seems so strange and such an unlikely thing, doesn't it? I shall never feel happy until we know how such a terrible accident occurred. Can Mr. Forbes help us, do you think?"

"I know," I answered with some hesitation, "that he meant to be here to-day, and I can't imagine what is keeping him. In fact, I don't know where he is. I do know, however, that he is taking a great interest in the matter, and—though I am not entitled to speak for him—I think you can trust him to find out the facts, if it is possible for any one to do so. I can only promise to tell him of your anxiety as soon as he returns."

"You don't think then," she added, "that he has any actual knowledge of what happened?"

"I can hardly say that," I replied. "I think he guessed at an explanation, and went away to put it to the test; but I would rather he told you himself if he has found anything unusual."

"Besides, mother," said Mary Cheney, "it isn't only the injection that seems unusual now, is it? You see, Mr. Kent, father went off in the afternoon, and left no word, and we had no idea he was going; whereas he would usually mention it to some one if he went away unexpectedly, and he was generally back quite early too."

"Still, my dear, we needn't worry so much about that," her mother answered, "for I've known it happen so, often before, and we should never have given it a thought if he had come home. But it would be a great relief if we could know. Mr. Kent, do tell Mr. Forbes how anxious we are, and say how grateful we are to him for putting himself to all this trouble. Come and see us as soon as he comes back, or no, we mustn't quite spoil your holiday with our anxieties, but at least send word when you can."

I promised to come and bring Forbes as soon as he returned, for I wished nothing better than to be of service
to them.

8

The Abandoned Mill

At half-past nine in the evening, after a dull, lonely day, I seized my candle and retired gloomily to bed. As I went to pull down the blind, I saw coming across the square, in his dark hat and caped coat, the figure of Horton Forbes. Overjoyed to see him, I dashed downstairs again, and greeted him like a long-lost brother.

He received my enthusiastic welcome with grave urbanity, in the manner of a great tragedian, and having remarked: "Procure for us both a sufficiency of whisky and soda, and the use of the only room," he proceeded upstairs with a stately tread. Soon we were snugly ensconced before a freshly lit fire, with the requisite supplies.

"And now," I said, "perhaps you will be good enough to explain what you mean by your disappearance, and what you have been up to all this time?"

"I will," he said, pouring himself a drink. "But it will be a long story, so let me hear your adventures first."

"My adventures!" I exclaimed bitterly. "I have not met with any adventures. However—"

And then I described the inquest—the result of which did not seem to surprise him—the funeral, and my conversation with Lady Cheney—at which he became thoughtful.

"Would you," he inquired, "say that Lady Cheney and her daughter are sensible people? Could they abstain, do you suppose, from gossiping?"

I indignantly repudiated the idea that they would gossip, and said they both struck me as very sensible indeed.

"In that case," he said, with a whimsical smile, as he raised his glass contemplatively, "it will be better to tell these very exceptional ladies the truth, although it is a task which I would gladly shun. However, it will give us a chance of learning more than we yet know, and that is very necessary. We can spare an hour or two to-morrow morning, and it need not detain us long. And now, as to my own proceedings. You recollect, no doubt, the paper which I found in the Professor's waistcoat pocket?"

I nodded.

"And the chess problem which I found in Shortditch's drawer? Which, by the way, you have not seen. Here is a photograph of it. Does anything about it strike you?"

"It looks to me pretty much like any other problem," I said, having examined it attentively, "except that white is in double check, which I should think is unusual. It is a little strange, too, that black has no pawns. But evidently it must be white's move, and only one move is open to him—K to Q3. The question is what will be black's reply to that?"

"That is not the question which is exercising me," Forbes replied. "For the move K to Q3 is impossible. I see you have overlooked something which I should have thought would catch the attention of any chess player. No doubt you will observe what I mean if you will study the board again. The conclusion follows that this is certainly no ordinary problem, but what it is I am at present unable to say. I thought it might be connected with the paper I found in the Professor's pocket, which read 2011325 Q. Sq.; for, considering that the Professor was found dead on the morning of March 12th, it was tempting to read 11325 as a date—March 11th. In that case, however, what was 20?"

"Perhaps," I ventured, "it might be the hour, reckoned in continental fashion?"

"Exactly," he answered. "I think it is. But Queen's Square was somewhat vague. I know of no such square in any place near here, and on the other hand, London, Manchester, Bath, and so on, seemed excluded by remoteness, assuming this note gave the hour and place where the Professor was to meet some one else for some purpose unknown. It then struck me that possibly 'Queen's Square' was a square on a chess-board, and I hoped by studying the chess problem to get some light on its position on the map. Unhappily, I completely failed. Beyond the fact that the chess problem is not a chess problem, I could not go.

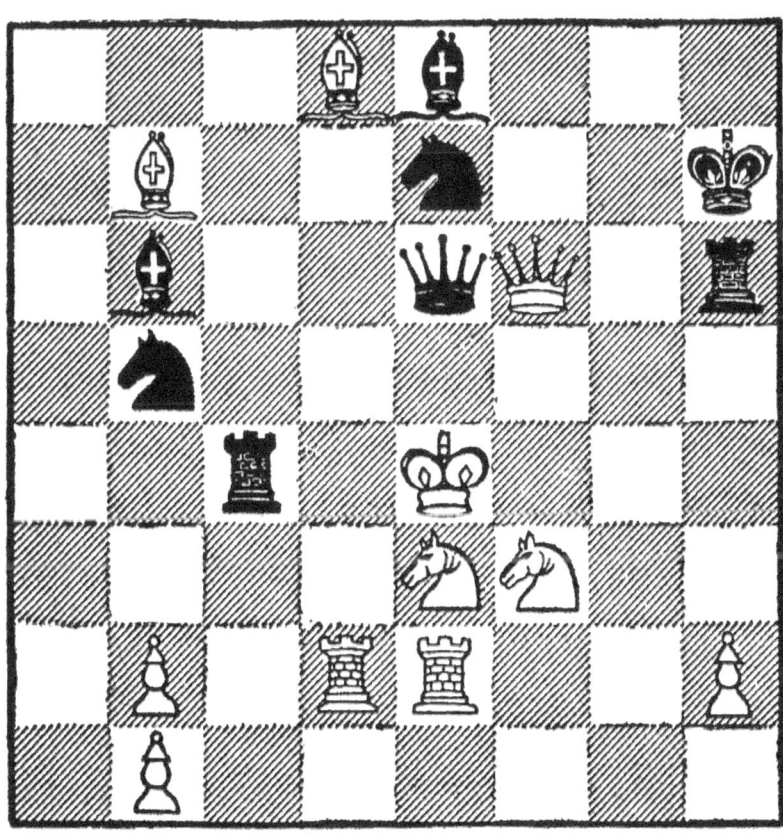

But if I was ever to go further, the way seemed to be by the unattractive Shortditch, who having produced one such effort, might produce or receive others, and thus enable me to compare and deduce. I decided to stick very closely to Shortditch, and to lose no time about it, for I thought that the discovery of Cheney's body might cause a visible flutter in the Shortditch dovecote, and the inquest, possibly, a flight."

"Before you go further, Forbes," I interposed, "I should like to have the solution of a problem that has been worrying me all the time. How did you discover any connection between Professor Cheney's death and the neighbourhood of Wilmer Station? I can see none even now."

Forbes tapped a long cigarette on his leather cigarette case.

"It was a psychological argument," he answered, pausing to apply a light, "and therefore very uncertain. A conjecture—but my only hope. My major premise was that no murderer, who has carried out an apparently calculated and cunning crime to within a hair's breadth of complete success, will choose that very moment to walk off, just before he can see his scheme's fulfilment. I felt certain that the man who killed Cheney and started the car on its course towards the lake, must have been compelled—doubtless against his will—to wait no longer, not even a moment. What could compel him? An intruder? Yes, at first that seemed the obvious thing. But consider; he had already done, evidently at his ease, all the incriminating work. There was no 'intruder' present when he started the car, or he would have left it alone instead. And now it was gone and nothing remained to connect him with it. If he heard sounds, or saw any one coming, he had only to withdraw into the shadow and watch the drama through.

"No; more probable than that seemed the supposition that he had, by the trouble with the car, already stretched his time to the utmost limit, and was obliged to get away from the scene of the crime then, or never. Now, as I had reasoned it, he had driven the car, and therefore had no other vehicle; the speedometer had shown a run of 62½ miles, from which I conjectured a return distance of about 30; therefore he must have an accomplice with a vehicle, or he was going by train. An accomplice, however, could wait one more minute. A train would not, and I decided in favour of that prosaic, but practical, explanation. The rest was merely due to Bradshaw. There are not many accessible stations, and very few early trains, and the 4.35 kindly simplified matters by passing without stopping the only other station from which our friend might have started, and—surprising, but true—the only other one, corresponding with the distance required, where he could alight."

"Now that you explain it," I said, "it seems to me to be perfectly sound reasoning, and to show great insight on your part."

"Hardly that," he answered, waving a deprecating hand. "It only shows a certain obstinacy in following a course of reasoning through, instead of half way, as one is always apt to do. The scoundrel was more anxious to get away before daylight and establish an alibi for himself, than to carry his task through, from which one might surmise that he was working for others rather than of his own accord, in committing the crime, and that he has a strain of cowardice in him.

"But to return to my story. The question was, how could I keep watch on The Laurels without exciting curiosity there or in the village? It was not in any case feasible, as you will remember, to watch both gates of the house from outside, and it was therefore necessary to invade the grounds. This, however, was rendered easier, I supposed, by the presence of the shrubbery, to which my attention was rather unpleasantly drawn the other day. It turned out, in fact, to be an even better refuge than I expected, for it runs right round three sides of the house, and is everywhere pretty dense.

"I entered easily by the tradesmen's gate, and turning to the right pushed into the shrubbery, in which I found enough clear space for walking, in fact, almost a suggestion of a trodden way. I was able, by stopping here and there, to get pretty clear glimpses of the house, though when moving I was unable to see it, on account of the thickness of the shrubs, which were chiefly laurels, as you would expect.

"When I reached the front gate, I took a close look at the room we were in the other day. It seemed to be empty, nor could I see any sign of life anywhere, beyond a wisp of smoke from the kitchen chimney. It was, however, something of a risk to cross the gateway in daylight, more particularly as the shrubbery beyond looked even more dense, and in fact impenetrable, and I decided to postpone exploration of it in that direction till I had exhausted other possibilities. I could see the whole of it from that point. It curved round the outside of the grounds, bounding a gravel path which ran at the edge of the lawn, until it was cut by the red brick wall, about eight feet high, which is the boundary behind the house. So I turned back, and when I came to the drive which leads to the house from the tradesmen's entrance—one is not at that point visible from the house at all—I easily crossed it, and made for the shrubbery the other side. I was baffled for a moment; there seemed no way in, and the trees there happen to be hollies, which are uncomfortable things to break through; but after a little exploration, I found a way further down, right by the gate, in fact. There, by squeezing close to a wooden fence, it was possible to get behind the hollies. After a few yards of difficult going, I was surprised to find a clear track, and one which, by the look of the ground, was still in use. It might be due to inquisitive children, of course, but at least it was there; it invited inquiry. It went meandering on among the shrubs for what seemed a hundred yards or more, and then ended, all of a sudden, at the brick wall.

"'This,' I said to myself, 'is becoming exceedingly curious, unless the Wilmer children really are inveterate trespassers.' However, I examined the wall carefully, but could see no trace of any one having climbed it, and there was no way round, for a certainty. I pulled myself up by my arms, with some effort, I admit, and found myself looking into a meadow containing a few cows. I next examined the fence, but equally without result. It was a solid wooden fence of the usual kind, vertical five-inch boards, tarred and set flush, not overlapping. I was on the outside of the fence, that is, the horizontal supports or transoms were on the other side, as of course were the stanchions, or vertical supports, and it was about a foot lower in height than the wall. There were no mudmarks or visible signs whatever that any one had climbed over, though I scrutinised it minutely, especially at the angle with the wall, where the path ended, nor of any door. Some strands of barbed wire fixed on top rather deterred me, but being an obstinate person I eventually pulled myself up enough to lean my head and shoulders over the other side, with my legs dangling against the fence.

"I was looking into a cobbled yard. Along the greater part of the left side ran a two-storied yellow brick building, which appeared to be a warehouse or mill. Opposite me was a double gate, once painted red, but now faded to a dirty strawberry, and closed by a rusty iron bar, pivoted in the middle and fitting into staples on each gate. A number of old empty casks were lying about between the fence and the nearest end of the building, beneath an open cistern, which had rusted into holes, together with sacks, iron hoops, broken bricks, bottles, and a pile of coal dust refuse. Grass grew here and there between the cobble stones. The place, whatever it was, was evidently unused, and seemed to have been locked up and untenanted for years.

"I was able, of course, to take all this in almost at a glance. It seemed scarcely worth climbing over at great risk to my clothes and person, and I was about to let myself down, when my attention was caught by a slight repeated rustling noise, which came apparently from the bottom of the fence just beneath me. With difficulty and discomfort I craned further over, and saw that it proceeded from a dead leaf which lay just up against the bottom of the fence. The fence, I then saw, was shaking slightly to and fro, and the leaf whispered the fact, and whispered also that the bottom of a stout fence can not ordinarily achieve the feat, being firmly fixed and immovable. There was then, a door, after all, or something at least which required investigation; and, sure enough, on exploring with my hand the upper transom, I found it undercut, and in the recess a small bolt! I withdrew this cautiously, though with some difficulty, for my weight was on it, and jumped down, as part of the fence, four boards wide, opened towards me, leaving the transoms in place on the other side. The hinges were fitted between the boards and the transoms, and were therefore invisible till the door was opened; but the whole thing looked like an amateur's handiwork, although it achieved its purpose of being not only inconspicuous, but quite hard to detect. But here was a distinct find—and a suspicious one.

"I passed into the cobbled yard, carefully bolted again the little door which I noticed was entirely invisible from that side also, and examined the building more closely. The end wall, facing me, was blank, except for a ventilator grating near the roof. The side wall, about forty feet long, had a door towards the near end, fitted, I noticed, with a Yale lock, and five bottle-glass windows on the lower storey. The upper storey was lighted, it seemed, by skylights, of which four were visible, all closed. The far end had a large double door, red like the yard gate, but again fitted with a Yale lock, which, though it did not appear new, was still not the original fitting, for a large keyhole had been filled up and painted over. Over the door was a window, now closed with a wooden shutter, which had evidently been used for lowering goods, sacks and so on, to the yard below, for the place where the tackle had been fixed was still visible.

"It is not easy to open a Yale lock off-hand, and I sought fruitlessly for any means of entry, first at the end I have just described, and then at that nearest the fence. I was just going to climb the brick wall which runs along the back of this old mill, or whatever it is, to try and get on the roof and through one of the skylights, when I thought I heard a faint sound across the fence. With a quickness on which I feel entitled to congratulate myself, I lowered myself—and to do it silently like that, was an ordeal— into the old cistern, and spied through a convenient hole. Hardly was I covered before a hand came over the fence, the little door opened, and in padded, on his rubber soles, our friend Fielding Shortditch.

"I could not see him after he passed the cistern, but I heard a key softly inserted, and a door gently closed. Very cautiously I emerged, and stationed myself just round the corner of the wall, whence I commanded every exit. There I waited for several hours. At last it grew dark, but still there was no sign or sound to reward my persistence. Stranger still, no light was visible inside. There was a faint sound, however, now and then, a kind of soft scratching. But it may have been rats or mice. Nothing seemed likely to be gained by further waiting, and I returned the way I came, just in time for the last train to London, which, naturally, got me there in the small hours, with the milk.

"In the morning I called on a friend of mine, Detective Inspector Channing, and told him the whole story. The police are instructed to keep an eye upon Shortditch, but to do so with the very greatest precautions against discovery, and to help us, in an unofficial way, of course, when occasion offers. So that I think we shall be all right in that respect.

"And now, before we go to bed, I have a proposal to make to you. Are you prepared to become, for once in a way, a housebreaker—or, rather, a mill breaker? To investigate that mysterious building is awkward for one, but 'when two go together,' as Homer says, it becomes a pleasure. What do you say?"

"Rather," I answered. "I'll come like a shot, but you must coach me in the part."

"Good," said Forbes. "And now you have shown your heroism by accepting, I must tell you that Mrs. Peck—that is Shortditch's brisk little housekeeper, with whom I have made rather a hit, I think—tells me he will be away to-morrow afternoon, so that will be our chance. We will go straight from Cheney Park. Personally, I would rather break into the mill than break the news to Lady Cheney."

9
PROFESSOR CHENEY'S SECRET

Cheney Park, although mellowed by the passage of two unhurried centuries, and beautiful, apart from that, in an unassuming way, was not a large house, or a large estate, and had so far escaped being overcome by waves of high wages and tempests of taxation, though larger and more imposing landmarks have long been quite washed away.

"Though your language," said Forbes, to whom I said something of this kind as we walked up the drive, "is rather rhetorical—with practice you might make a politician, only you must learn to mix your metaphors more—I agree with the sentiment. It's a really charming place, and I only wish we came on a more cheerful errand. It is a shame to bring bad news on such a delightful morning, to such a delightful place."

"And," I said, "to such delightful people. I can imagine no earthly reason, can you, why any one should have wished to murder Professor Cheney?"

"I can imagine several," he answered. "But I have no idea whatever, as yet, what the true reason may be, though I hope to learn something this morning which may give us a clue. They have a new gardener, I see. That man is not accustomed to handling a spade."

By this time we were approaching the house. Near the right end of it was a fine old cedar, and to our left, across a green stretch of parkland sprinkled with beech trees, lay the lake, sparkling where the breeze stirred it into ripples, and beyond it rose hills purple-brown with trees in bud, though as yet leafless. The house itself was partly in shadow, for it faced southwest, but a gleam caught an old sundial on the wall. As we came nearer, in a little yard at the end of the house, we saw Mary Cheney feeding some pigeons with corn which she was throwing out of an Indian silver bowl. She made a very charming picture, and looked very fresh and sweet in spite of her black dress— or perhaps because of it—as she came forward to meet us. I introduced Forbes, who assumed a certain old-world courtliness for the occasion, and said:

"These are some of your pets, I expect? Fine birds, and in fine feather. That, I see, is an Archangel, and that a Jacobin. What is this fellow?"

"I think it is a homer," she answered. "But I don't really know. It was one of father's birds, and I have had them all to see to since he's gone. But if you will excuse me a minute, I will go and find mother. She will be very relieved to hear that you have come. If you wouldn't mind going round to the front door, I will send Emily to let you in."

At the door, however, we were met by Lady Cheney herself, who greeted us with marked cordiality.

"It is very kind of you to do all this for us, Mr. Forbes," she said. "And you too, Mr. Kent. You ought to be having a good holiday after all your hard work instead of being worried with our troubles. But tell me, Mr. Forbes, have you been able to learn anything about my poor husband's death? It was such a dreadful shock to us to hear what the doctor said, because we felt certain that my husband would not have used that drug himself. How can the accident have happened?"

"Allow me to say first, Lady Cheney," he said gently, "how very deeply we feel for you, and to assure you that we are both most willing to do anything possible for your peace of mind. But I am afraid— However, perhaps you will allow me to ask you a few questions first, for I am still a good deal in the dark."

"Willingly," she answered. "Shall we talk indoors, or stroll about the garden? Mary dear," she added, turning to her daughter, who had just rejoined us, "will you fetch my shawl? I left it in the dining-room, I think. I love these spring mornings," she went on, as she wrapped the shawl round her shoulders, "but the wind is treacherous, isn't it?"

"Did Sir William, before he went out in the car, receive any letter, or message of any kind?" Forbes asked.

"None," she said, "as far as I know. There were certainly no letters that day. I remember that. And no telegram. We have no telephone in the house. I didn't hear of any one bringing a verbal message, but I will ask the maids."

Inquiry showed that no message had come to the house, and as the Professor had remained indoors all day, except when he went out to the pigeon loft, as he usually did just before tea, it seemed that no such reason could account for his sudden journey.

Forbes then asked: "Can you explain at all why he decided to go out so suddenly?"

"It was not very unusual," she said. "He did sometimes go out like that after tea. He used to smile at me when I asked about it, and tell me not to be inquisitive."

"Can you tell me," said Forbes, "what friends Sir William was in the habit of visiting?"

"There were not many, I think," she answered, "whom you could say he went to see regularly, although, of course, we knew most of the people round here, more or less, and he would call on them from time to time. There was Stanley Deeming, at Clunford, you know—they were very old friends, and at Cambridge together—and Mr. Drummond-Cavendish, at Norton Cheney—we got our Sealyham from him, that was how my husband began to know him well, and they used to discuss Plato—and who was that German, dear?—oh, yes, Hegel. I must confess I never took very much to Mr. Cavendish, but perhaps that is only because I am a jealous old woman, and he took up so much of my husband's time. And less often he would go over to Kingwick to see another old friend, Sir Laurie Wilmot. But, of course, if he had been to see any of them they would have let us know: and indeed I cannot imagine how anybody who saw him that day can leave us like this and not tell us so."

"Yes, it is very strange. Did Sir William ever mention a clergyman, Mr. Fielding Shortditch?"

"Never to me. Have you heard the name, Mary?" But Mary shook her head.

"Then please don't mention my question to any one at present," said Forbes. "Did Sir William, do you know, ever attend meetings of any society or club?"

"Well, he belonged to several societies, scientific and literary, but I think he has not attended many meetings of late years. We are rather far away from such things here. He used to go to Shrewsbury about once a month, but that was all I remember."

Here Mary Cheney made a movement as if to speak, but checked herself.

"He was, I believe," continued Forbes, "a distinguished chemist. Did he do any work of that nature here?"

"Yes; he had a laboratory, which I suppose I can show you now, though he would never let us enter it, and even now I have not been inside it myself. He had been very busy there for some weeks before his death, but I never asked about it, for I knew he liked to make a little mystery of it with us."

"I think I ought to see it, for his own sake, Lady Cheney," Forbes said, gently. "But I will go alone, if you will show me where it is."

"It is kind of you. Yes, I will take you to it. Mary dear, take Mr. Kent and show him our little rock garden."

"Do, please, Mr. Kent," Mary said beseechingly, as soon as the others had gone, "do, please, tell me what Mr. Forbes really thinks. But perhaps I ought not to ask you? Perhaps he has told you not to say?"

It was hard to resist the pleading look in her eyes, and yet it was hard also to tell her.

"On the contrary," I said, "he wants you to know, but he would be glad to spare you the knowledge. The fact is—well, he thinks—and I am afraid it does look like it—that there has been foul play."

"Oh! I knew it, I knew it," she cried, bursting into tears. "Poor, poor father! How could they do it! Oh, Mr. Kent, please don't think me silly, but I was so fond of him—I am so fond of him. I knew what had happened as soon as ever I heard what the doctor said, but I couldn't, couldn't believe it."

I took her hand and tried to calm her, and expressed my sympathy in such clumsy way as I could. In her agitation she had forgotten about the rock garden, and we were standing by the edge of the lawn, near a clump of rhododendron bushes. Presently she went on:

"Do, please, tell me what you think. Father, you know, was a very clever man and a great chemist, but he was as simple as simple could be, and he used to love having some little secret which he thought nobody could discover. And he was very fond of me, and sometimes he used to share his secrets with me. The last time he seemed more than usually in earnest, and he told me a secret which, he said, was of tremendous importance, and made me promise faithfully not to tell a single soul, ever. Ought I to tell? Not even mother knows yet."

At this point I thought I noticed a rustling among the rhododendrons, and if a secret was to be revealed, one could not be too cautious, so we moved away.

"You know what it is," I answered after reflection, "and can judge best, but if it could have any bearing on your father's death, I think you ought to reveal it. If you tell me, I promise not to let it go further than Forbes, unless it is vitally necessary."

"Well, I will," she said. "It is for father's sake, and I am sure he will forgive me. What he said was: 'I have discovered something tremendously important, which, if rightly used, will make war impossible. But the difficulty is that if my discovery were wrongly used nothing can describe the horrors it would cause. I have revealed the existence of this secret only to a very few whom I can trust, and who have sworn and pledged themselves to use the discovery only in the interests of humanity, and I mustn't say more than that.' And he made me promise solemnly never to mention what he told me to any person on earth."

"I am certain, Miss Cheney," I said, "quite certain that you have acted in the spirit of your promise, and that your father would certainly approve. This means nothing less than that your father's secret was the prize which the 'friend' who killed him was playing for; and Heaven help us if he got it!"

"Oh! what can we do!" she exclaimed. "It is awful, horrible to think of all poor father's lifework being turned to what he hated most! Mr. Kent, can't the police do something? Can't they get hold of this awful man and stop him?"

"Of course," I assured her, "the police are doing, and will do, whatever can be done: Forbes and I—not that I count for much—are heart and soul in this affair, and between us, I have very little doubt that we shall succeed. Don't worry unduly, my dear Miss Cheney. I am sure it will all come right."

"Thank you, again and again," she said. "You give me hope, at any rate. And I think Mr. Forbes is splendid. He is so—regal; no, not quite that—more Olympian. I mean, he seems so capable and calm and unperturbed. Is Mr. Forbes—is he a detective?"

"No, I don't think so," I answered. "Not, I mean, by profession. It is a kind of hobby, I think. But he is certainly clever, and astonishingly quick at reasoning things out. I don't believe you could find a better champion, even if you went to Scotland Yard."

"Forgive my intrusion," said Forbes's voice behind us. "So you have heard, Miss Cheney?"

"Yes," she answered. "And I knew, really, all along, that there had been foul play, but it seemed impossible to believe it."

"Naturally," he replied. "Your father was a man whom no one could have had reason to hate. With regard to Scotland Yard, I have already been there, and put a friend of mine, Inspector Channing, in possession of all the facts, so far as I had learned them, so you may be assured that everything is in capable hands. And now, Kent, we must be preparing for the next move. By the time we have walked back to the village, we shall be almost due to start."

We walked together back to the house, took our leave of Lady Cheney, and then set out on our way back. I gave Forbes an account of Mary's promise to her father, and told him what the secret was. "The Professor said," I told him, "that he had discovered a secret which would make war impossible, Forbes. Startling enough, wasn't it?"

"Now I wonder," he murmured reflectively, "what can have become of that gardener? You see, he has left this bed half dug. Not a case of new brooms, apparently. I am sorry, Kent. Don't think I was not attending to what you have said. On the contrary, your discovery is the most important that has yet been made. It gives us a convincing motive, and a direction for our search, which I hope we may be able successfully to follow. Did the Professor indicate the nature of his discovery?"

"Apparently not," I answered, "or at least I was told nothing of it. But what have you found out?"

"I have discovered," he said, "that Lady Cheney and her daughter are, as you said, very charming, old-fashioned people. Miss Cheney appears to me to belong to a past age, which, personally, I greatly prefer; and to have its graces without its defects. Her evident love for her parents seems to me to be very well deserved."

He would say no more about our case, but talked instead about the Stuarts and their tragedy.

10

The Gladstone Bag

When we got back to the "White Hart," Forbes went up-stairs to his bedroom, while I refreshed myself with a glass of beer at the bar. In a minute or two I heard something being dragged bumping down the stairs, and perceived my usually indolent companion struggling with an enormous Gladstone bag, which had evidently done much duty, but yet was inscribed in staring white letters with the name J. Smith-Ponsonby and seemed heavy enough to be full of gold plate. "For Heaven's sake, Forbes!" I said, "you have not started burgling already, have you?"

"Rather an indiscreet question, Kent," he answered, as he reached the level, and deposited the bag, "considering the unquenchable curiosity of Mrs. Huggins. But, no. This contains merely a few little requisites for our expedition. My scheme is to go in my car as far as Bucknell, effecting certain alterations in our appearance on the way; to leave the car there, and proceed by train. Give me a hand with this as far as the garage." We struggled along together.

"Wouldn't it be somewhat simpler," I said, "to go by car the whole way?"

"Yes, but this is not America, and we are still so primi-tive that even yet it is not usual in country villages for the braziers and the locksmith to drive to work in a six-cylin-der saloon car. It might attract attention. It is regrettable that the British workman so seldom wears corduroys now-adays, for now there is nothing left to show that he does work, but I did the best I could. Our outfit will at least be sufficiently different from our usual dress to have petrified Mrs. Huggins, if we had put it on here."

We reached the garage. The car was soon brought out, and we heaved the bag in. Forbes took his place at the wheel, and we started on the short run of some six miles. There was next to no traffic on the road, and it was easy to find a quiet stopping-place, and to change our clothes in the car.

I was astonished at the multiplicity of unexpected and extraordinary things which the bag disgorged, and for which, in many cases, I could see no possible use. First, for instance, came a basket of pigeons; next a small coil of rope, in the centre of which were two electric torches and two automatic pistols; then two workmen's baskets full of tools, and a brief-bag. Beneath these came two pairs of black felt slippers, and the clothes, which we proceeded to put on. Forbes then stained my face, neck and hands with some kind of cosmetic, resembling a stick of shaving soap, which produced a dirty, sunburnt colour, and I did the same for him. We then replaced the rest of the things in the bag and drove on.

"What are the torches for?" I asked. "Are you intending to stay in this mill all night?"

"I sincerely hope not," was his answer, "for Shortditch is supposed to be coming back to supper, and I shouldn't wonder if he were to pop in. It only seemed to me that if no light could get out of the mill, possibly none could get in."

"That's true. But aren't we being rather lavish in our preparations? I mean, all these tools, and the pistols? I can't think Shortditch is quite so formidable as all that, and I doubt if he will have the pluck to meet us at all, don't you?"

"It would be a great mistake to underestimate him, Kent. His cunning may be greater than his courage, but the way in which he disposed of Cheney shows that we ought to be prepared for both."

"Why, I thought he bungled that badly. Anyhow, he left enough for you to trace him by."

"Yes; but only by the sheerest accident. Have you considered how much we should know about him, but for that accident to the carburetor? No? Well, nothing at all. The car would have disappeared under twelve feet of water. Although anxiety about the Professor might have been felt next day, it is almost certain that a day or two would have elapsed before a hue and cry was raised, and probably much longer before it occurred to any one to search the lake—even if that were ever thought of. And then what clue could have been found to suggest murder? Not one of the facts I noticed could have had the least relevance—all signs of the injection would probably have disappeared—the radiator would have been cold, and no argument could have been drawn from the engine, the lights, the gear, or the steering. Even if, for some reason, some one suspected, I can imagine no way by which they could trace the crime to Wilmer Deeping, without knowing, as I did, the time when it took place. No, it was luck, or destiny, which defeated Shortditch. Though, of course, we may say it was his fault in so far that, in his excitement, he used an unsuitable instrument on the carburetor, and used it unthinkingly. But here we get out, and leave the car."

So saying, he turned the car on to an open space by the road, a little way out of the village, where we left it, and walked to the station.

"I have arranged with a man here," said Forbes, "to drive it on for us, and leave it at a garage just out of Wilmer, but it is better for us to go by train, although we can

come back by car. We shall then not arouse curiosity till
our object is accomplished."

We had left the Gladstone bag, and were now only carrying the workmen's baskets, and the pigeons, about which
Forbes would give no information, except that he thought
they might possibly come in handy.

At last we arrived at our destination, without having
excited any apparent interest, and proceeded to reconnoi-
tre, taking the tradesmen's entrance to The Laurels as our
starting-point. Immediately to the left of this gate was a
by-road, which I had not before noticed, leading, according to a slanting and defaced finger-post, to "Little Deeping 3 miles." We followed this for a hundred yards or so,
and then saw on our right the high brick wall and faded
red gates of the mill—as we agreed to call it, in the absence of other information. Beyond was an open field. The
wall all round had broken glass on top, and the gate was
equipped with rusty nails. We noticed that it was impossible to see part of the wall from the road, so that it would
be possible to climb up there fairly securely, but finally
we decided not to risk the glass or the nails, but to get in
by The Laurels' shrubbery. We did so with considerable
circumspection, but without accident, passed through the
cunning little door, and, creeping stealthily to the building, listened for any sound inside. We heard nothing, and
decided to make a start. It was by then about half-past
three.

"We do not propose," said Forbes, "to enter by the door,
but, like the wolf, by some other way—I think, the roof."

"You disappoint me," I answered. "All the detectives I
have read of have always been equal to opening any lock
on earth in about four minutes."

"We are but human," he said with majesty, "and I think
the roof will be much easier, and less noticeable. So let us
begin with that. But first—our felt shoes."

We removed our boots, which we put in our baskets; then, Forbes leading, we easily scaled the wall at the corner of the building, by climbing on the old cistern. As we walked softly along the gutter we found that the skylights were just level with our heads.

"Ah! this should be an easy one," said Forbes, stopping at the second. "You see the top corner of the glass is broken off. We will try."

He produced from his bag a glass-cutter's diamond, and drew it firmly over the glass along the frame, leaving a deep scratch. Next he took a punch, and a light hammer, and tapped gently along the scratch, with the gratifying result that the glass cracked cleanly and gradually along the whole length. After working round three sides, he called me to his assistance, handed me a pair of leather gloves, and told me to catch hold of the broken corner, and to hold the glass hard to prevent its falling. This was successfully accomplished, and the whole pane came cleanly out, leaving an opening about two and a half feet by eighteen inches.

We looked through it into a large attic, as it were, running half the length of the building, from the rest of which it was separated by a brick wall having a door in the middle. The walls were plastered, there was no ceiling, and the place was completely bare. The floor of rough boards was about seven feet below the skylight, and entrance was perfectly easy. I went first, and Forbes handed me our paraphernalia, and the frame of glass, and then followed. Next he inserted at each corner of the window frame a small thin piece of iron between the glass remaining fixed there and the putty, so as to project about a quarter of an inch, and then replaced the glass we had removed.

"No one will notice it has been taken out," he said, "unless they look closely. On the other hand, if we want to get out suddenly it will not hinder us."

We now proceeded to examine our surroundings. The door in the party wall was locked, but the lock was an ordinary builder's fitting with a drop over the keyhole, and we left it for future investigation. Across the room, almost opposite us as we stood under the second skylight, was a narrow wooden staircase, with a handrail down the wall. We descended it, and found that near the bottom— there were sixteen steps in all—it curved round to the left, and presented us with the obstacle of another locked door—and this time with a patent lock.

"Dear me," exclaimed Forbes, "our friend is provokingly secretive. I am not going to tackle this lock, Kent, except as a last resource. This door must lead us beneath the room we have just left. Let us see first whether the floor above would not afford an easier means of entry."

We therefore retraced our steps and examined it. It had originally consisted of good solid planking, but this had fallen into bad condition, and, in some places, pieces had been replaced. Forbes went to work at one of the weak spots, and soon had a couple of planks up, quite large enough to get through. The screech of the rusty nails as they came out was startling and disturbing in the stillness.

A surprising sight greeted us—for here again there was no ceiling, and nothing to obstruct the view—namely, absolute blackness. Simultaneously we switched on the torches which Forbes had so thoughtfully provided. They threw a bright circle of light on a luxurious Persian carpet, and the corner of a deeply padded divan.

"Come," said Forbes, "this is a most stimulating discovery." And without more ado, he lowered himself through the hole, and I quickly followed, dropping some five feet; but no sooner had I landed on the soft carpet than an awful thought struck me. How were we to get out again?

About this, Forbes was gently satirical, having happened by some chance to observe that the locks, which

presented only a small slit on the outside, were provided
on the inside with an easily manipulated milled knob, so
that we had merely to open the door and walk out. That,
as he suggested, was the method which he himself would
probably follow, but he assured me that he did not wish
in any way to cramp or confine my inventive powers, and
would be pleased if I chose to depart through the floor or
in any other way that might take my fancy.

11
THE ROOM WITH THREE DOORS

Forbes's first action, once we were within this exceedingly
comfortable room, was to open the door leading to the
staircase which he had just descended, go upstairs and re-
place, without nailing them down, the floor boards which
we had removed. Next he collected all our kit with certain exceptions, including the rope and the mysterious
pigeons—tied them up firmly with stout string, and
ascending through the skylight, hurled them violently
over the wall among the bushes. On his return he replaced
the glass of the skylight for the second time; the pigeons
and the rope he left in the empty attic.

"Really, Forbes," I said, "I do wish I could begin to
understand your actions, and why you do this and that. If
you had left it to me, the first thing I should have shied
away would have been those infernal pigeons. And what
the deuce is the use of that coil of rope? Are you proposing
to hang Shortditch, or what?"

"Your questions, my dear Kent," he replied urbanely,
"though undoubtedly apposite, are nevertheless inoppor-
tune. Let us rather use our time, which may be precious,
in investigation of our enemy's position, rather than our
own; and first, to prevent surprise, I suggest that you
might open that other door, and take up a strategic position in the doorway."

This was a door fitted like the other with a milled knob, and leading towards the front half of the mill, and it was brightly illuminated, at the moment, by Forbes's torch. Growling a bit at his secretiveness, I did as I was ordered, opened the door, and switched on my light—to start back immediately with an exclamation of astonishment.

"Good Lord, Forbes," I cried, "come and look at this!"

We were looking into a large space, with a brick floor, occupying all the front of the building, and in it our torches showed the back of a large limousine! There could be little doubt now that it was Shortditch whom we had seen at the station that evening—Shortditch, who devoted his money to other uses, and had never learnt to drive!

All the windows in this room, as well as in the other, were made of thick greenish glass and covered over with American cloth, and admitted no light. We switched on the car lamps, which lit up the place sufficiently to show us several cans of petrol and oil, a large water can, and a bench for repairs. Forbes noted down all particulars of the car itself, which was of an American make, and then turned his attention to the contents; our most striking find seemed to me to be that of two different number plates in one of the lockers. Forbes, however, was much more interested, apparently, in some maps which he found in the dashboard tray. He pulled them out, one by one. "H'm! Dunlop Map of the British Isles—the usual thing— nothing much to help us in this. Ordnance Survey, scale of a quarter inch, Sheet 8; the same, Sheet 7; the same, Sheet 11. He is well provided, anyhow. Ah! this is different—yes, I see it covers roughly the same country, but what a small scale! One in twenty! Why, it is smaller in scale than the Dunlop! I wonder what he wants this for? And he uses it, too, a fair amount, judging by the wear, and marks of dirty fingers. Look, here is a little circle in red ink—you see, just at the intersection of those lines which form squares—let me see—yes. Kent, I believe we have struck oil here! Look, here is another circle—and here another—and here a fourth. Most remarkable—all at an intersection, and all—by Jove, yes—Kent, just jot down the positions of these circles carefully, will you, as I read them out?"

I hastened to comply, for Forbes seemed quite eager about it, though as far as I was concerned, I was again at a loss to know why he thought this so important.

"Good," said he, when this was completed. "Well, I think we have learnt as much as we can here. Ah! but wait! What about this luncheon basket on the carrier? One might possibly discover. . . . H'm, yes, a curious meal—still alive, apparently. I rather suspect . . ."

At this point, having lifted the lid cautiously (for the lock was a simple one), he disclosed twelve beautiful pigeons. Concealed beneath the plumage of each of them was a tiny aluminum case, embossed on the centre of which was a black mitre.

"It is odd," he continued. "I expected to find them, but not to find them here. Well, let us see if we can learn anything further elsewhere. Now, if you will take up your position in the doorway, you will be able to give warning of any one coming by the main door. As to this side door, as it opens direct into the room I have to examine, the only thing to do is to put the catch on the lock." This he did.

"Why not do the same with the others?" I suggested. "Then we'd be safe from interruption."

"Yes, but at the price of revealing the presence of intruders, which it is better to avoid. I don't want Shortditch, even if he comes back while we are here, to have any suspicion of our presence. But about the side door we have no choice. We must merely hope that he will not try to come in that way while we are in the room."

While speaking, Forbes was lighting a paraffin lamp, which stood ready filled and trimmed on a large, leather-covered writing-table. From my station at the door, which was at the left of the room as I looked into it, and immediately at my left hand, was the side door leading into the yard. In front of me was the large writing-table, facing the covered window, with a leather padded office chair, and beyond it the projection in the wall which concealed the staircase. Along the far end of the room ran shelves holding bottles of chemicals, partially hidden by curtains. The centre of the floor was unencumbered, and the divan was set with its back to the writing-table, and was flanked by two deeply padded easy-chairs, the table with the type-writer being at the near end. There was no fireplace, but instead a stove with an asbestos brazier to burn vapourised paraffin. At my right hand was a cupboard containing drinks, glasses, and so on.

As I took all this in, Forbes was prowling all round the room, looking at everything, but with a dissatisfied expression. At last he returned to the typewriter, and began examining some carbon sheets which lay beside it under a glass paper-weight. Presently he gave a soft exclamation and, holding one of the sheets up to the light in his left hand, sat down and wrote on a pad which he took from his pocket.

"This is a piece of luck, Kent," he said, replacing the things. "This happens to be a new carbon sheet, and the type of a message is legible. So is the date, which, it is interesting to note, is 12325. And this, is the message:

"'At our tournament Lake yesterday, playing on no mere formula, arranged surprises now and then. Q. Kt. to Q. Sq., for instance, came in well, and really finished the game by preparing for discovered check. It disposed also of the threat to the Queen. The game will be long remembered, and special report sent you, probably by post on

Sunday.' Why did Shortditch type this here instead of at the house?"

"I don't know," I said. "But to me it simply suggests that Shortditch is genuinely keen on chess, and runs some village club. Lots of parsons do. I don't see how it helps us."

"Does a genuine enthusiast, in sending out problems to a village club, show the board upside down? Yet that was the case with Shortditch's problem, as you will see if you refer to it again. Here it is. And why should a conscientious parson send out reports of chess tournaments by post on Sunday, of all days? Ah! I see you have noticed that pawn at last! What do you think now?"

"A cipher!" I exclaimed.

"Obviously," he answered. "The only question is whether the problem happens to be the key to this particular message. It is probable enough, for a chess cipher is likely to be complicated to construct, and so sparingly used. Let me see what I can do."

Meanwhile, perhaps through having nothing to do but stand and listen, I began to feel unaccountably nervous. Behind me was pitch dark—in front the closely sealed, thickly carpeted and dimly lit room. There was heavy silence everywhere. I had never felt the slightest fear of Shortditch, but the feeling of dread and apprehension which now crept over me was akin to that deep terror which is sometimes felt in dreams, and seemed equally groundless. It was like a mist rising sluggishly in my soul, and casting over my spirits an inexplicable shadow. More than once I restrained myself from urging Forbes to make haste and get away, but fortunately for my self-respect, I refrained.

At last he got up quietly and put back the two papers in his pocketbook. "I think I have got the key to it, Kent," he said, "and I should like to get it to Channing without delay. We are too late for the post, but you might catch the train up to town this evening. I was going to propose that

you should go up to-morrow morning in any case. I have
discovered that this mill was bought by V. S. Stephens, of
21 Paradise Street, Barking. But Mr. Stephens appears to
have lost interest in it, and so I feel a good deal of interest
in him. You will find things in the Gladstone. Leave me
an address."

I sat down, wrote that address, "Lincoln Hotel, Berners Street," with a pencil from the tray, and handed it to
Forbes, who was busy making a copy of the message. He
gave it me, with a photographic print of the chess problem.

"It is quite easy to decipher," he said. "All you need to
know is that Black takes precedence over White, and black
squares over white squares. A touch of the devil about
that! And it gives us conclusive evidence against somebody, and proves the existence of an accessory. As to the
writer, circumstances point very strongly to Shortditch.
Hush! What was that?"

A key was being inserted, very softly, in the main door.
In an instant, I was in the room, and had closed the door
silently behind me, though the sudden shock imparted a
certain quiver to my fingers. Equally quickly Forbes had
blown out the lamp, and using our torches sparingly, and
without a sound, we made for the door to the stairs. We
only barely reached it in time, being delayed by Forbes
inserting a probe in the keyhole to enable him to close
the door behind us, and it was impossible to avoid a slight
click as the bolt sprang home. But we wasted no time to see
if we had been overheard. "Up, quick," whispered Forbes,
in my ear, "tread firmly and keep close to the wall."

We managed it without mishap, although I feared at
every step that the stairs would creak and betray us, and with
an equally catlike softness we stole over the floor above. I
was making for the skylight, but Forbes caught my arm.

"Not yet," he whispered, "there is more to do. Lie down
on the floor by those boards we lifted, and see if you can

raise one enough to look through, while I attend to the lock on this door. But only if you can do it silently."

I did as directed, and with extreme caution inserted my fingertips in the space at the end of the board and raised it an inch or two. The lamp had not been relighted, but there was an occasional gleam of light, apparently from the place where the car was, so that the intervening door was evidently open. Soon this light advanced into the room beneath me, and was seen to come from an electric lamp, which its owner set on the writing-desk, bringing into the light as he sat down the flabby features of Fielding Shortditch. It was still not much past five, and we had not expected him before seven. From some small object which I could not see, he extracted a slip of thin paper, and spread it out, and began studying it side by side with another slip from his pocket case.

Just at this moment, Forbes summoned me, and I heard a slight click as the lock turned. Forbes picked up the basket, and handed me the rope, and we passed through the door, closing but not locking it. At last I began to understand. The place was a pigeon-loft, and in it were a dozen birds, already going to roost. On each of these birds was a little case exactly like those we had already discovered, with the exception that in several instances the figure embossed on it was a black crown. Forbes seemed to be puzzled, and fingered the thing reflectively. "What do you make of it?" he asked me. "In the car twelve pigeons with the monogram of a black mitre; here six with the black crown?"

I shook my head. "I hardly know what to suppose, unless they are marked differently because they come from different people."

"That is the obvious explanation. But are those in the car just arriving, or just going away? It may make an important difference. However, to be on the safe side, I will take both emblems to decorate my birds, which I will leave here to bring us what news they may."

He effected the change quickly and deftly, and had hardly put the last of the stolen birds in our basket when, with an unpleasant thrill, I heard a key being very softly inserted in the lock of a door almost immediately below us. I plucked Forbes's arm, and was for making for the skylight, and getting away while there was still time, for I had very little fancy for being caught by Shortditch messing about with his pigeons, to which evidently some mysterious importance was attached. But Forbes made light of it, and refused to budge.

"This may be just our chance," he said, and going to the shutter, which formed an ingress and egress for the pigeons (as I have said, it was of good size, having formerly been used for lowering goods) he raised it an inch or two. This enabled me to see that it was the main doors which had been opened, and in a few seconds the bonnet, and then the whole, of the car came into view—pushed out by some one whom we could not see, but whom we supposed to be Shortditch. It was just dusk, but still light enough to notice that the yard gates were ajar, so it appeared that the car was about to leave. However, having pushed it clear into the yard, the person behind it left it there, went back into the building and softly closed and locked the gates behind him.

"Magnificent!" Forbes whispered, jubilantly. "You see the pigeons with the black mitre are being taken away in the car. That means that their home is here. And these with the black crown belong to the person to whom Shortditch sends his messages. We must track that car to its destination at all costs and you must postpone your visit to London till tomorrow. Let us go."

He opened the shutter, threw the rope, already knotted together at the ends, over a staple above the aperture, and swarmed quickly and quietly down it. I threw him the basket, and followed.

12

COAL DUST

The tracking of the car seemed to me to present no particular difficulty, considering that Forbes's own car was waiting about a quarter of a mile away; but there was no opportunity for the moment to point out this obvious solution, because we had to concentrate our attention on getting away without being discovered. This our felt slippers made a comparatively simple matter, and we passed into the shrubbery without being observed, and thence into the wood adjoining the mill. There we retrieved our goods and chattels from various bushes into which they had fallen. I then remarked to Forbes that personally I proposed to do our tracking by car, but I should be quite agreeable if Forbes preferred to walk or fly, or to pursue the car in any other manner that might take his fancy.

"Ha! do you bite your thumb at me, sir?" he said. "I admit your right to retaliation, but honestly I don't think your plan as feasible as it seems. If I drive without lights I can make no speed. If I have lights, I can hardly escape observation, and yet keep the other in sight on a winding country road. Is there nothing we could fix to the car which would leave a track?"

"We might stick something on the tyre—or what about tying one of those empty sacks under the luggage grid, and letting it sweep the road?"

"Not bad. But no use on a clean road. Here's a better idea: let's fill one of those sacks with coal dust, and have a little game of hare and hounds. We can slip in through the front gate and fill the sack. Then you can leave it to me to fix, and make the necessary arrangements, while you take these things, and bring the car to the end of the lane, where I will meet you. You'd better take my card to the garage, or there may be bother about getting my car."

We decided to carry out this plan, and I soon had the car at the appointed place, and not much too soon, either; for hardly had I been there five minutes before the limousine came silently down the lane. As it turned into the main road, where I was waiting in Forbes's car, a street lamp showed me the driver clearly. He was a young, respectable-looking fellow in a dark green livery, a typical chauffeur—and he had no appearance of being on any unlawful errand, or of being in any hurry. But further thought of him was cut short by the immediate appearance of Forbes, whom I had not expected for some minutes. He explained, however, that he had tied on the sack, so that it would work loose, and fall off when empty; getting right under the car and lying flat on his back in order to do so. While he was in that undignified but inconspicuous position, the young chauffeur had strolled in, whistling, opened the gates, got into the car and started. Forbes, as soon as he was free, clung on to the luggage grid, and so travelled. He had a bad moment when the car stopped immediately outside the gates, and the man got out to close them; but he dodged round the car, and as the man evidently was not suspicious there was no real difficulty.

By this time the tail light of the limousine was just disappearing in the distance, so we started off, using the side lights only. These were not strong enough to show the road in detail, but it was only necessary to switch on the headlights to distinguish a thin black line of coal dust on the white surface. The road at first was exceedingly hilly and twisting, and then ran down into a valley and along a stream for some miles to Aberllyn; then after a little difficulty in picking up the trail, for three turns—one to the left, and two to the right—occurred in succession, we found ourselves on a by-road which ascended steeply and continually for seven or eight miles, and seemed to be leading us into more and more wild and desolate surroundings. All round us towered great bare hills, their long outlines showing black and grim against the stars, with one specially high peak which dominated the country to our right.

"A mysterious destination this, Kent," said Forbes, breaking a silence which had fallen upon us as we climbed. "Our general direction seems to be southeast, and we have come already nearly thirty miles. There seems to be no probability of any kind of habitation in these wilds, and it looks as if we shall have to go nearly as far again to reach one. In that case I am afraid we shall lose the trail."

He switched on the headlights again—as he had done at intervals—but the thin black line was still discernible. We were climbing up an especially stiff gradient just then. A few minutes later we rounded a steep curve between high banks covered with withered grass and ling, and came out on a level stretch, and then began to descend, though much less steeply than we had ascended. After a time, the faint sparkle of running water became visible on the right—a mountain brook, the course of which we followed for some miles, and which grew in volume as it fell, until it became a narrow but rapid stream. The road was straight, so that we could see it faintly white ascending what appeared to be a terrifying hill in front of us, the rise beginning about half a mile away; but just at the lowest point, beyond a bridge over the stream, there were four cross-roads. Our black trail now seemed thicker than ever—it was, in fact, the last of the dust which had run out more rapidly than the rest. At the cross-roads we were obliged to stop, and examine the signs on foot; but at first we could find none. Then I discovered that the trail ended just short of them in a little conical heap of coal dust.

"So, he stopped here, at least," said Forbes. "It is something to know that; but it is most exasperating that our trail should fail us just where we want it most, after wasting itself on miles of simple road. We cannot even tell how long the stoppage was, for this seems to be the very last of the dust. The question now is, which way to try? There seem to be no tyre-marks—at least none are visible by this light, though they must exist. If I made my knot right however—I was a bit hurried—the sack ought to have fallen off before it got much further. We had better pick the most likely road and explore."

We considered the possibilities. Straight ahead, the road, which at a distance had seemed good enough, now proved to be not much more than a cart track, rutted and apparently grass-grown. It did not seem likely that a car could have used it. Between the other two ways there seemed no choice; but as the heap of dust was rather to the right of the road, it seemed more probable that the car had been preparing, if it was to turn at all, to turn to the left. So left we went, and sure enough not a quarter of a mile on we found the sack lying tumbled on the grass—presumably thrown there by catching the wheel. The sight of it revived my flagging spirits. At first the excitement of the chase had kept me going, but when the scent failed, and we had to take to our feet—for we left the car at the cross roads, on the grass—I suggested to Forbes that it was really hardly worth going further. We knew the car's number; wouldn't it be quite as simple to find out its destination by that means?

"Certainly," he answered, "if we could be sure that its present destination is the registered address of the owner. But I think we can hardly assume that; and in any case, inquiries made in that way would take some time, and the information might come too late to be of use. Our object, too, is not so much to find where the car goes, as what becomes of the pigeons."

"How did you know," I asked, "that pigeons came into the plot, and that Shortditch would have them? You seemed so sure of it, yet I can't see why."

"Obviously," he answered, "Professor Cheney's expedition was connected with the slip of paper which I found in his pocket. He left home in time to keep that appointment, and never returned alive. How did that paper reach him? There were no letters that day, or the day before, which was Sunday. No one brought him a message; but he visited the pigeon loft just before tea, and left immediately after it. He was in the habit of visiting his pigeons at that time. It was easy to guess that the message reached him by that means. Therefore, if he kept pigeons to enable some other person to communicate with him, it was probable that the other person kept pigeons for a similar reason. In fact, as soon as pigeons were mentioned, I remembered the soft scratching I heard at the mill. It seemed a fair inference that there was a regular pigeon post in existence, and events have confirmed it."

"Yes, I follow. But why is it so important to trace these particular birds?"

"I am acting on the supposition," he explained, "which I think is a reasonable one, that the black crown is likely to be the device of the chief of this gang, and if so, it would be a great score to be led straight to him by following Shortditch's birds, which appear to be sent in exchange for his own. But of course, that may not be the fact.

Instead of a direct exchange, it may be a case of passing birds on round the gang, in which case we should find only a subordinate—if indeed we find any one at all. Unfortunately, in actual fact these things never work out as simply as they might on paper."

"I begin to see the idea," I said. "You think the gang are known to each other by symbols taken from chess? But still I don't see what need there is for them to use all these mysterious methods. Especially the pigeons. Why not send messages by post, or even by hand? If it's necessary to fetch these pigeons back by car, surely it would be less trouble to send their messages by that means in the first place?"

"All those objections," he said, "seem to me quite sound, up to a certain point. But there are two things to be said; first, that this seems mysterious to us, and reminiscent of the penny dreadful, because our first sight of it has been of the seamy side. We connect it in our minds with the Cheney episode, and Shortditch. But in plain fact, there is nothing at all out of the way in, say, a country gentleman being at once a chess enthusiast and a pigeon fancier. Dozens of them are both. Nor would it be inexcusably eccentric to combine the two hobbies, by sending chess problems by pigeon post to others of like tastes. Indeed, I will say this, that if without having any ideas of a crime to trouble you, you were to come across such a country gentleman with his chess and his pigeons, you would think it the most natural thing in the world.

"Secondly, we have the advantage over the reader of the penny dreadful, because we have the facts before us. We know that these people do in fact employ this unusual device—at least, we are sure enough—and therefore, that they must have some reason which appears to them sufficient for doing so. Several reasons occur to one. They may, for instance, want to give the very picture of themselves, which I have just described—as simple harmless people with two well-recognised and inoffensive hobbies. They may wish to avoid revealing the interconnection between them which might appear if letters were sent and received by post. And they would have a still stronger reason if their names and addresses were unknown, even to each other—which is not an impossible supposition. Indeed I think it quite likely that the leader may keep both entirely to himself."

We had now reached a point where the stream, of quite considerable volume by this time, rejoined the road, but now on the left-hand side, and at a greater distance. A little further on, was a drive leading presumably to a house, and at the entrance a quaint little square thatched cottage, with squat windows and one chimney, looking like the witch's cottage in a fairy book. A little beyond it, some distance off on the left of the road, was a square tower; and between this and the road was a collection of nondescript buildings, one of which had a water-wheel worked by the stream. As far as we could judge, the buildings were derelict, having been connected with some quarry or mine which had been abandoned.

Apart from these, there was no sign of any other habitation, nor of the car. Forbes was for making a thorough investigation of these derelicts, but one has to draw the line somewhere. We had already, in my opinion, done more than enough for one day; I was ravenously hungry, since it was now half-past seven, we had had no time to eat since lunch, and I was determined to get home as soon as possible. The idea of going to London had, of course, been abandoned long since.

"Well," Forbes replied to my objections, "perhaps you are right. Still, one never knows how unfortunate it may turn out to miss a chance when you have it. I admit,

though, that it's too dark to see much; also that I am as
hungry as you say you are. But at least let us try whether
we can learn anything at this cottage."

I felt constrained to agree to that, and we walked back
and knocked at the door, which was opened by a pleasant
white-haired old lady, who seemed to have some difficulty
in understanding what we said. We had, I ought to mention, resumed our collars and ties, and were wearing hats
and overcoats. Forbes inquired whether any cars were
likely to pass that way, explaining that we had lost ourselves and wanted to get to any place—no matter where—
from which we could get a conveyance. Shaking her head
at this, in a bewildered way, the old lady called "John!
John!" Whereupon John appeared from the kitchen, mop-
ping his face with a towel, and in his shirt sleeves. To my
delight, I at once recognised him as the chauffeur who
had driven the limousine. So of course did Forbes; and we
both kept a pretty keen eye on his face when Forbes repeated his question to him. But there was not the slightest
sign of anything suspicious; indeed, if I have ever seen an
honest open face, it was his. There was no sign of cunning
in it, and not much intelligence; but it suggested a person
who would carry out orders faithfully, and without questions or curiosity.

"There's hardly a car on this road, sir," he said, "not
from one year's end to another. It don't lead anywhere
much, sir, you see."

"And yet we thought," I said, "we noticed a car's tracks
just now."

"Ah! yes, sir. That would be our car, sir. Mr. Francis's
car, sir."

"Indeed," said Forbes. "Do you think there is any
chance that we could prevail upon Mr. Francis to befriend
two weary travellers?"

"I am very sorry, sir; but I am afraid not, sir."

"Could we see Mr. Francis?"

"I am afraid it is quite impossible, sir. Mr. Francis dis-
likes strangers, and we have strict orders, sir."

"Oh, well! we must make the best of it. Come, Kent!"

"All this is rather odd," he added, as we walked back to
the car. "I shall have to investigate that house, with Mr.
Francis's consent, or without it. But we can do nothing to-
night, and it will be just as well to allay any suspicion by
withdrawing for a time. I will go back to Worcestershire
to-morrow, where I hope to get some further information,
and you can take the first train to town, and see Channing. I will look round this place as soon as possible, and
we can meet again in a day or two."

But if we had known what the future held for us, we
should have parted with more misgiving.

13

THE CIPHER AND THE KEY

Untroubled by knowledge of the future, it was with quite a holiday feeling that I caught the first train to town next morning. Horton Forbes, for his part, moved to a cottage of his in Worcestershire from which his pigeons had been sent. He intended to be on the spot to receive any messages which his birds might bring in, and also to continue the investigations of Mr. Francis's house which we had to abandon the night before.

For the time being I had had enough of it, and I was not at all sorry to exchange the excursions and alarms of the country for the peace of Piccadilly. And as for improving my acquaintance with Mary Cheney, I seemed just as likely to be able to do it in London as in Luttercombe, where life was so strenuous that there was no time even to eat.

It turned out after all that I reached Scotland Yard in time to see Inspector Channing. It was a visit which I had rather dreaded; but what struck me most about Channing was the absence of a stiff officialism. Perhaps Forbes's note may have had something to do with it, but Channing himself was the sort of person who puts you at your ease. He had a long, square-jawed face, clean-shaven and rather brown; grey-blue eyes, with a humorous twinkle; dark, curly hair, and in everything a suggestion of the sea. One felt that he would be more in his natural environment as a hand on a yacht or a mate on a large liner, than in a London office.

He read Forbes's note with a comical expression of profound thought, which was caused by raising his eyebrows, and so producing across his forehead a series of perfectly straight furrows.

"Well," he said, when he had finished, with a friendly sort of grin, "we fellows up here will be out of a job soon between the pair of you. Now, this is my busy day, because I'm going off duty at twelve; but if you don't spin it too long, I can give you two shakes of a duck's tail."

Thereupon, I recounted our adventures and discoveries as briefly as I could; and summed up by saying that we seemed, as far as I could make out, to be up against some kind of a gang, who used a cipher and sent messages by pigeon post. One member, probably Shortditch, had murdered Cheney for an important chemical secret. I did not explain further the nature of this secret.

Channing did not, as I half expected, make fun of the whole thing; but on the other hand, did not seem to attach much importance to it. Nevertheless, his attention and penetration were shown by the quickness with which he summed up the case as soon as I had finished presenting it to him.

"Mind you," he began, "I don't say that old Horton Forbes isn't perfectly right, and on to a real thing; but there's one thing I do see sticking out a yard, and that is that you haven't got a shadow of evidence. Granted that the Professor was murdered, which is not yet proved; and granted that Shortditch might have done it, and might have made that track from the line, what evidence is there that he actually did so? All we know about him is that he was at home as usual at 7.30 p.m., and fast asleep in bed at 7.30 a.m. There is no proof that his occupation of the old mill is for any illegal purpose. There is no proof that the chess problems are not what they seem to be, or that they are not perfectly innocent. It is no crime to carry pigeons in a basket, and Mr. Francis is perfectly entitled to dislike strangers, and to give strict orders that they shall not be admitted."

"That," I interposed, "is just what Forbes wanted me to see you about. As a matter of fact, though we haven't yet proved the guilt of Mr. Francis, we have proved, at any rate, that the chess problems are not innocent."

Here I laid before him a copy of the chess problem, and the message about the game of chess.

Channing glanced at the problem and read the message aloud:

"At our tournament Lake yesterday, playing on no mere formula, arranged surprises now and then. Q. Kt. to Q. Sq., for instance, came in well, and really finished the game by preparing for discovered check. It disposed also of the threat to the Queen. The game will be long remembered, and special report sent you, probably by post on Sunday."

"Well," he said, with a smile, "these are both very harmless, on the face of them. What conclusion has Forbes drawn?"

"The conclusion that the problem is the key to decipher the message. I worked it out myself in the train, using one or two hints which Forbes gave me. After a bit of difficulty at the beginning, I found it absurdly easy."

"But you might have found it much less so," replied Channing, drily, "if you hadn't had the luck to secure, not only the cipher, but the key as well. Scarcely any secret could resist that combination long. But as far as I am concerned, this one is still intact. So go right ahead and explain."

"It is very simple," I expounded, with considerable relish of my position. "You first of all write the message in lines of eight words, so that they correspond with squares on a chess board. Then you take the Black King, and pick out the word corresponding to his position. This gives 'Q. Kt.' Then the Queen, which gives 'came.' After that, the rest in order; and where two are equal, take the black square first."

Channing took a pad, and wrote rapidly, picking out words one by one. Then he said: "Is this what you got? 'Q. Kt. came Q. Sq. yesterday now finished and disposed of in Lake formula will be sent you by special post Sunday'?"

I agreed.

"Who is Q. Kt.," he asked, "and where is Q. Sq.?"

I explained.

"Right," he said. "This is quite enough to be going on with, and we shall act accordingly. I take it that Forbes is not anxious for any immediate arrests?"

"No, entirely the contrary," I assured him. "He wanted you to be convinced of the real existence of a conspiracy, so that you would be prepared to act, if he found sufficient reason to suggest it."

"Tell him we shall. Now is there anything else I can do for you?"

"I don't think so; unless you can tell me anything of one V. S. Stephens, of Paradise Street, Barking—the fellow, Forbes says, who bought the building Shortditch is using, about a year ago."

Channing wrinkled up his forehead and reflected; then he picked up the telephone.

"Do you know anything of V. S. Stephens . . . Barking? What? . . . L.C.C? Righto!" Then turning to me: "He is a pretty well-to-do aniline dye manufacturer, owns a good deal of house property, is a member of the L.C.C. and other public bodies. Stood as Labour member last election. I guess that's all out of *Who's Who* or somewhere, so you can verify it for yourself, but he seems to be on the square, right enough. Still, if you're not satisfied you can get to Barking from Charing Cross in about half an hour."

Feeling rather foolish, I took my leave, and once outside, turned my steps in the direction of Piccadilly, while uneasily trying to persuade myself that to go to Barking was absurd and yet walking as if I meant to walk there for a wager. It was a lovely spring morning, and such parts of London as have not been renovated into the appearance of a pretentious suburb were looking delightful. I was walking up the Haymarket, deep in thought, when suddenly I cannoned into a "man about town" who on turning round revealed the well-remembered nose and cheery countenance of my old friend Riverton.

"Why, why!" said he. "My dear old thing, I am delighted to see you and all that, but why butt into my back? I mean, what about going round me to wherever you are going to? And likewise, where are you going to?"

"Jolly to meet you again after all these years," I said. "And—well, the fact is, I was thinking of going to Barking."

"Barking," he exclaimed. "Oh! no, no. My dear old fellow, no. It's off, definitely. Why, you'd miss your lunch. I mean to say, breakfast in Barking—probably; beer in Barking—yes; but never lunch in Barking. It simply can't be done. Now there is within these confines a certain hostelry I wot of yclept Ye Goate. Come round there and have one—or perchance two—and afterwards we will feed somewhere. The Barking move is cancelled."

"All the best people go to Barking nowadays," I said, "or if it isn't Barking it's somewhere equally remote. However, for the sake of old times. . . ."

So it came about that I found myself seated with this friend of war days, in a Regent Street restaurant where, over an adequate lunch and a bottle of excellent Pommard, we seemed to renew some of the spirit of cheery irresponsibility which used to be the charm of "leave."

Riverton, after demobilisation, had got a job of some kind in the Home Office, which appeared to suit him very well; he knew any amount of people, being, as I have said, a sociable and genial soul. And some pretty odd things he could tell of some of them, and did tell too, a little later on, over the coffee and liqueurs. Our conversation had naturally turned to the curious adventure in which I was—so accidentally it seemed—involved, and he showed a much more lively interest in it than I expected. For one thing, he also knew Horton Forbes—they were both, as it happened, members of the Attic Club—and he knew of some of the people whom Forbes had mentioned to me as missing.

"For instance," he was saying, "did you ever come across that exceedingly odd and somewhat noisome old bird who called himself Caspian Orme? Rummy sort of name, but I suppose he gloried in it—a johnny with a face like a vulture and a lot of very dead-black hair? Disappeared one day from the dear old home, if you remember, and took a little nest egg of a million or so with him—or some one else did—but anyhow it was a queerish show. He came home from somewhere—China, people said—and started splashing about a bit, and painting the landscape more or less red down those parts. And the people he had in his house! gadzooks and also oddsfish! they were a crowd. But the rum thing was that Mrs. Brook-Sutton—you know Mrs. B. Sutton. Not know Mrs. Brook S.? Well, well! Then this child will put you wise, or in other words, expound. Mrs. B. S. is pretty hottish stuff. She had been on the same lay as old Caspian—a sort of queen of that particular push. Every one knows of her. She has a large place down in Gloucestershire and goes in for revel and riot and wine and what not. Anyway, she sailed in one day, and then old Caspian's work was done. They met at Mrs. Burling's one night—and I happened to be around—and spotted it. Like a snake looking at—what's the jolly old beast I mean—ah! an ichneumon—sort of 'do I bite first or do you' expression they had. After a bit, however, they seemed to pal up together surprisingly, for as I was sitting out of the giddy throng, smoking and so on, out came Mrs. B.-S.—by the way she is still devilish good-looking, though she has had time to get over it—with her arm in Orme's, and deep in friendly talk. 'Absurd man,' she was saying—you know how she does her ravishing smile—oh! no. Still never mind: 'Absurd man! In a country where everybody looks after their neighbour's morals! Why, it's certain.' Then they saw me and shut up like oysters. However, the point is, that dear old Caspian disappeared almost immediately after that, but though I've racked the old bean for an explanation, I haven't got it. But it all seemed deuced odd."

"It is rather queer," I said. "What about the lady; did she disappear too?"

"Bless you, no—no, no, far from it. If possible, she stepped higher than ever. Seemed to have even more cash and even less conscience, if you get me. And in fact, I don't mind saying, some fellows have got into a pretty considerable mess over it—what with binges and cards and what not. Young Barclay, for instance, at the Foreign Office—simply gone all to pieces since. . . . Still, that's his funeral. But, of course, she knows half the big pots in town, and seems to be able to twist 'em round her fingers. Absolutely rotten, the whole thing. And the extraordinary blunders fellows seem to be making. If you were in my show you'd think the same. All the wrong men seem to get the jobs, and the right ones seem damn well to do the wrong things. Well, let's drop it. What about coming down this afternoon for a bit of golf?"

"Sorry, old man," I said, "but I think I really must go to Barking. After all, that's what I'm here for."

"Noble valiant youth," said he, "shalt go alone into the wilds of Barking? Never! the faithful Riv. is with thee. We will embark together."

14

THE CHAUFFEUR'S STORY

For the average person, Barking itself is the Ultima Thule; and Paradise Road seemed as remote as Paradise itself; for it was on the furthest outskirts, and led us through dreary flat land near the Roding, which even now is beyond London's furthest coast. The house we were in search of proved to be a new building of uncompromising ugliness, standing solitary and unashamed; but within hail of a factory, on the wall of which was painted in dingy lettering, "V. S. Stephens & Co., Aniline Dye Manufacturers."

As it was Saturday afternoon, however, the factory was now closed for the day, and I was spared any necessity, which my conscientiousness might have caused, to investigate it. Moreover, it was a relief to have Riverton with me. He would convey to any one that we were merely a couple of silly asses from the West End who were out to browse in Barking, and so suspicions—if there were any—would be disarmed.

Everything about Mr. Stephens's house was exceedingly proper. The lace curtains were nicely looped back; the aspidistra occupied the exact centre of the window; none of the bits of coloured glass in the front door were broken; and there were no cigarette ends around the gas fire. "A modest but refined home, old top," said Riverton. "Your friend Stephens is the kind that made England great."

He had at least made himself great, as we soon found when his cockney maidservant presented us to him—in fame and achievement possibly, in size certainly. He was tall and also large, and even then he appeared to be not contented with his boundaries, but to be stretching them still to their utmost limits, thereby putting no inconsiderable strain on his skin. Riverton chose an apt adjective in describing him as an "inflated man." His face was florid, his hands large, and his manner assured, if not overbearing.

"Well, gents," he said, "what's your business?"

"I came to inquire," I said, "whether you own a certain property, which according to my information, is the case, in Wilmer Deeping. . . ."

He stared at me. "And why does that interest you, may I ask?" he inquired, in an uncivil tone.

"If you do own that property, sir," I said, rather irate, "I'd like to inquire if it's let."

"I've no property to let down there. What is it you want?"

"I was informed that you owned a mill or warehouse there which is believed locally to be unoccupied."

"Then you were informed wrong. And again I say, what is it you want? If you want to do business with me, I'm open to do business. But I'm not open to discuss my private affairs with those as they don't concern."

I was getting distinctly the worst of it, and scarcely saw how to proceed. After some hesitation, I decided to play my last card.

"The fact is," I said, "that interest has been aroused by the recent discovery that this mill, which is to all appearance and belief unoccupied, is used by a certain person in a manner suggestive of secrecy, and the police are suspicious. I have just come from Scotland Yard. . . ."

"You belong to the Yard?" he snapped at me.

"No," I answered. "I went there to—er—consult a friend."

"Then you'd best go back and tell your friend at the Yard that if your friend at the Yard wants to inquire into what property V. S. Stephens owns or lets, and what he don't own or let, he can damn well come himself, and I'll tell him."

"I say, dear old friend," said Riverton, "hold on to the old wool. I mean to say, no need to get snappy, what? As touching this ruined mill now—what we are asking ourselves is, how much do you want for it?"

"Well, if you're a buyer, you might have said so earlier. I've no wish to sell; but if you like to make me an offer, I'll think it over."

"And what about vacant possession? Could we get it?"

"Yes, at midsummer. It's let at present to some party, whose name I don't recollect. But you'll excuse me, gents, if I tell you that this isn't the way I do business. If you want the mill, make me an offer in writing, and I'm open to consider it. Good day to you."

"Well, well, well," said Riverton, as we closed the gate. "A genial soul is Stephens. He's the lad that put the bark in Barking. One of the bulldog breed. And now it's me for courtly Kensington, and cheery Chandos Road."

I had certainly got very little for my long journey and my trouble; but at least it appeared that Stephens did own the mill, and that a tenant was legitimately occupying it. This, though most unsatisfactory from our point of view, was a new fact at any rate, and Forbes possibly might be able to use it. I returned to my hotel—I was staying at the Lincoln, in Berners Street—and having removed the grime of Barking, prepared to spend the rest of the time in a rather more pleasant manner.

On Monday morning I received by the first post a letter from Forbes. "Dear Kent," it ran, "One of my birds has just brought me a useful little piece of information, and what is more, a formula in what I believe to be the Professor's

writing. The county police are now convinced that murder
was committed, by evidence which will no doubt be revealed at the adjourned inquest; but they have no proof of
the murderer's identity. Please yourself, of course, about
coming down here. There is nothing much for you to do
at the moment. If you cared to stay a day or two in town,
quite possibly you might be able to learn something about
V. S. S. or the others, but do just as you like."

I was a little surprised therefore, when in the afternoon
of the same day, on returning to my hotel after tea, I saw
Forbes's car standing outside. Naturally I went straight
into the hotel, expecting to find him there waiting for me,
but I looked for him in vain. Then a page came up and
told me that the chauffeur of the car outside had an urgent
message for me. I went out. The chauffeur was standing by
the car, and I noticed that he had kept the engine running.
I had an impression that I had seen the man before, when
I was in Forbes's company, but I could not exactly place
him. I had little opportunity, however, to consider this
minor question, because the message which the man had
to deliver was of so unexpected and terrible a kind that my
heart stood still at hearing it. Mary Cheney was missing!
This was an overwhelming blow. The very disaster, which
I had hoped to make impossible by agreeing to help Forbes
in this case, had occurred; and all my confidence in myself
collapsed, and my faith in Forbes was severely shaken. By
what incredible folly or oversight had he—had we—allowed our enemies the opportunity of doing this? For that
it was their doing it never occurred to me for a moment to
doubt. But what was to be done now?

"Who are you?" I said to the chauffeur. "What does Mr.
Forbes want me to do?"

"I am Lady Cheney's chauffeur, sir," he answered, respectfully, "and Mr. Forbes's orders was that I was to ask
you to come back with me immediately. If you will step

in, sir, I will explain as we go along. I was to say, sir, that every moment is of value."

Without even pausing to collect my things from the hotel, or to settle my bill, I got into the car, which immediately started westward. As we traversed at good speed the comparatively quiet streets to the north of Oxford Street, the chauffeur began his story.

"Yesterday morning, sir," he said, "Miss Cheney received a telegram from Mr. Forbes in Worcestershire, which her ladyship gave me to show you."

He produced it, and I read: "Will you come identify your father's writing? Will send car for you noon to-morrow." This evidently referred to the formula which Forbes had mentioned in his letter to me.

The chauffeur went on with his story.

"Miss Cheney was unable to reply, as there is no post out after noon on Sunday, as you know, sir, and the telegraph office likewise was closed; but she intended to comply with Mr. Forbes's request, and was expecting his car on Monday at twelve. However, at about nine o'clock, it would be, a car of the same make as this one drove up to the house—very like this car it was, sir—and after a few minutes Miss Cheney came out, and entered into conversation with the driver. After that she went back into the house, and a few minutes later, she came out again, ready for travelling, got into the car, and it drove off. I was occupied in the front garden, sir, at the time, and as the car came down the drive, I observed that the chauffeur was a young chap that I have often seen about. Before coming to Cheney Park, sir, I was employed in a garage at Wilmer Deeping. . . ."

"At Wilmer Deeping!" I exclaimed.

"Yes, sir, and this young chap used to drive a big car to and from The Laurels. I informed her ladyship of this fact, and she appeared to become rather anxious and

worried, and to doubt whether that would be the car which
Mr. Forbes had arranged to send. She said she would wire
to Mr. Forbes and ask, but I suggested that Lady Cheney's
car would take me to him as quick and asked if I should
go over and inquire. She instructed me to do so, because if
Mr. Forbes happened to be out I might be able to find him,
or to inquire from some person whether he had sent the
car. Accordingly I did so, and arrived to find Mr. Forbes's
car just preparing to start, according to his telegram. The
car had not been sent by him, sir."

"This is terrible," I said. "Heaven grant that we may
find her! What plan did Mr. Forbes propose? Had he any
idea how to trace that car?"

"Well, yes, sir, but not for certain. The young chap
told me that he was employed by a Mr. Francis, sir, but I
was not aware where that gentleman lived. But Mr. Forbes
appeared to know, and his plan was that the distance not
being very great he would drive over there in Lady Cheney's
car, which as you may know, sir, is not so fast as his own,
and that I should bring his car up here to fetch you. It was
his opinion that the lady might be in some danger, and he
thought it better to have your help. In the event of his not
being able to find the lady at Mr. Francis's house I was to
say that he would meet you at the cross-roads which he
said you would know, sir; but if he was not there, you were
to go to the house, enter by the side door, which would be
left open, and wait in the first little room on the right."

"Yes, that is very clear," I said. "It is most fortunate
that you noticed the driver of that car. We shall owe you a
good deal if we find Miss Cheney."

"Thank you, sir. But if I may say so, sir, I should have
said that the matter is not a very serious one. Mr. Forbes
may have his reasons, but the gentleman at The Laurels is
a clergyman, and the driver of that car is a very respectable young chap, all above board, sir."

"Well, I hope to God it is," I said.

"Are there any suspicious circumstances, sir?" he asked me.

His curiosity was natural, but I thought it better not to gratify it incautiously, and merely replied that Lady Cheney's anxiety in the matter was sufficient reason for treating the circumstances as suspicious until we had an explanation of them. And there our conversation ceased. The chauffeur was competent, and though I was burning to get to our destination, I had no reason to complain of the speed which he maintained. It was a dull, gloomy afternoon, with a northeast wind, and an appearance of imminent rain, which never fell, and my depression of spirits was not lightened by looking at the colourless landscape and the leaden sky as the great car hummed along the Oxford Road. By the time we had arrived there it was already dusk, though we had done the distance in two hours from London. We turned off in the direction of Gloucester. As darkness fell, and roadside trees and hedges, lit by the glare of our headlights, took on the appearance of scenery in a theatre, starting suddenly out of nothing into strange and grotesque shapes, something of nightmare was added to the oppression of the central fact that Mary Cheney had been tricked into the hands of a murderous gang. When we had passed Gloucester, and went on and on into the ever more lonely and rugged country across the river, my impatience grew upon me so that I could scarcely sit still in my seat.

We reached the cross-roads at a few minutes after eight, and stopped there for a minute or two. There was no sign of Forbes, and the chauffeur twice sounded the electric horn, but nothing stirred. This ought to have been consoling, as indicating that Forbes had found Mary at the house, and that everything was well; but I was unable to rid myself of the foreboding that the explanation might be that something had happened to Forbes. And so, it was with no sense of relief, but rather one of extreme anxiety, that I directed the chauffeur to drive on to Mr. Francis's house.

The little, square, one-chimneyed cottage by the gate—which, I noticed, was open—looked more witch-like than ever in the pale light of our lamps, and then vanished behind us as we swung up the drive, between tall yew hedges, plentiful but untrimmed. The drive was longer than one expected, and curved round to the right; and as the house—a long low building—came into view, the square tower showed up dimly against the dark sky quite close to it.

We passed the front door, and stopped opposite a small door in the side of the house. As Forbes had said, I found it open, and this to some extent relieved my mind. Inside was a narrow stone passage, dimly lit, with one door at the left and one at the right. That on the right was ajar, and was evidently the one intended, but as no light came through the opening I concluded that Forbes was not yet there. Striking a match I pulled the door open, and stepped in, when, to my horror, the floor gave way beneath me, and I fell downwards through empty space.

15

The Unlocked Door

After the first shock of terror and surprise, and the awful feeling of falling, I waited for the crash. But with a gasp of relief I realised that the floor once more felt solid beneath my feet. Something was checking my descent, and very soon afterwards, with only a slight jar, the motion ceased. Bewildered, but restored to control of myself, I fumbled for my matches, and struck a light. Its feeble glimmer showed me that I was in a cellar of some kind, with a solid brick floor, on to which I stepped and looked about me; but just as my match began to burn itself out, I heard a slight rumbling noise behind me and turned round. I was just in time to catch a glimpse of the lift—for that was what it was—reascending. I made a wild grab at it, but miscalculated in the darkness, and stumbling over something, fell heavily.

When I had recovered from this further shock, and picked myself up, I expended more matches examining the lift shaft, with the object of finding the rope by which it was controlled, but if this rope existed, I was unable to discover it. The sides of the shaft were of brick, and there was no sign of any rope, or of anything else of the kind. My light was far too feeble to show me the height of the shaft, which appeared merely as a pit of blackness, some four feet square. My heart rather sank at this, but I was

not yet seriously alarmed; supposing that there would no
doubt be some perfectly easy way of remedying my stupid
mistake, as I imagined it to be; and, in fact, I was suddenly struck with the ludicrous similarity of my descent
to that of the demon king in a pantomime, and burst out
laughing. But my laughter came back to me in a muffled
echo, which was slightly chilling, and restored my bal-
ance. So I proceeded, at considerable expense in matches,
which might better have been reserved, to investigate my
surroundings.

The cellar in which I stood was fairly spacious and
lofty, with a rounded roof, like that of a tunnel, and ran
transversely. There was a small grating high up in the end
wall to my left; a solid door opposite me in what would be
the side of the tunnel; and in the right end wall an open
archway. The brickwork was all whitewashed, and solid
shelves ran most of the way round, the lowest being about
two feet from the floor; and from the fact that a good part
of them were occupied with household articles, which I
did not notice more particularly, I inferred that the cellar
was still in use.

I first tried the door opposite me, but it was fast. Knocking on it produced no result. Striking another match, I
passed through the arch at my right, and found myself in
another cellar, exactly like the first—the wine cellar, it
seemed, from a large number of empty bottles still lying
on the shelves. There were also, rather strangely, groceries
of various kinds; among which I was delighted to find a
couple of candles. The discovery was opportune, for when
I had lighted one, I had only one match left. I tried the
door leading out of the side of this cellar, but like the
other, it was immovable; nor was there any other way out
to be found. I beat on these doors, first with my hands,
and then with a tin of pressed beef—which was the best
instrument I could see—but with no result. I also shouted

as hard as I could, in the hope that the sound might pene-
trate through the gratings; for the masonry and doors were
too substantial to give any hope of making myself heard
through them; but there was no reply or sound in answer.

Finally, returning to the first cellar, I re-examined the
shaft by which I had come in. It had the appearance simply of a large chimney, with one vertical metal bar let in
on each side for the lift to run on, but there was no sign
of apparatus by which the lift could be controlled, and the
shaft was too large to climb. Temporarily, at least, I was
a prisoner, and I cursed myself for my stupid blundering.
I must have mistaken my instructions. It must have been
the door on the left which I should have entered, not that
on the right. Yet I felt fairly clear that it was the right the
chauffeur had said. Perhaps the mistake was his. At this
point a very unpleasant thought crossed my mind—and
setting up the candle beside me I sat down on one of the
shelves to consider. Was it possible that the chauffeur's
message had been a hoax, and that I had been entrapped
deliberately? If so, I was in a remarkably nasty position,
and very likely an extremely dangerous one. But then an
idea occurred to me which brought me considerable consolation. If the message was a hoax, at least there was no
longer any reason to suppose that anything had happened
to Mary Cheney. That had been merely the bait to get me
into the trap, I thought. Was this not far more probable
than actual kidnapping? The latter had seemed to me quite
inexplicable all along; for she had made no move to track
down our adversaries, or to hamper them in any way, and
could scarcely, surely, be a danger to them; nor had I yet
been able to hit upon any reason which could make such a
dangerous expedient worthy anybody's while.

As for myself, however, I supposed that I might have
excited more suspicion perhaps than I knew; the gang perhaps thought that I had learned more than in fact I had,

and considered me a dangerous enemy. And this would be
a very good place, I reflected, for putting an unwanted
person out of the way. No one, I knew, had seen me step
into the door on the right; no one so far as I could tell,
was aware of what had happened, and there seemed quite
a chance that it would be impossible to make any one
aware of it. In that case, I should starve eventually, unless some other fate were reserved for me. And yet, I felt
very unconvinced. The theory that the message was a hoax
did not seem to fit at all. In the first place, the chauffeur
had told his story so simply and convincingly; I had had
no doubt of its truth, in spite of its startling nature. Secondly, how explain Forbes's telegram? That again seemed
perfectly genuine. It referred, clearly enough, to the formula which he had told me he thought was in Professor
Cheney's handwriting; it had been sent, as the postmark
showed, from his Worcestershire cottage—or at least, from
the nearest office to it—and it appeared improbable to the
last degree that any one could have obtained the requisite
information in time to fake a telegram, considering that
according to his note to me written on Sunday, Forbes had
said he had "just received it himself." Further, it seemed
impossible to explain how Forbes's car came to be sent—
there was no doubt at all that it was his—unless he himself
sent it; and what finally clinched the matter, and proved
to me beyond dispute that my hoax idea was impossible,
was that, except for Forbes and Riverton, no one knew my
London address. So, Riverton, being out of the question,
there was no one who could have known where to send the
car but Forbes himself, and that being so, it followed that
there had been no hoax; that my present position was due
to accident simply, and, unhappily, that Mary Cheney was
missing after all.

    Why, I reflected, even at that very moment she was
probably somewhere in the house, possibly in need of my

help; and springing up in desperation I began again to wrench furiously at the doors, and to seek fruitlessly for any means of escape. I even tried to scale the shaft, and by putting my back against one side, and my feet on the other, I managed painfully, and with great exertion, to hoist myself a few feet up; but after slipping and falling several times, I had to abandon the attempt. Bruised, tired and disheartened, I sat down again, and looking at my watch, found that it was nearly ten o'clock. I was very thirsty, and hungry as well, so I set about looking for something to eat and drink, although with no great hope of finding much in a cellar. But I was pleasantly surprised. There were several varieties of tinned foods, including fruit, and a plentiful supply of wines and bottled beer, so that anyhow the danger of starvation was remote. With the aid of my pocket-knife, I made an excellent meal of pressed beef and beer, followed by peaches, and then broached a bottle of port.

A good deal refreshed, I set about looking for means to make myself comfortable for the night, since it seemed vain to hope now for any release till the next day. In this, again, I succeeded far beyond my expectations, for in the other cellar I now found almost everything that necessity could require. If preparations had been made to receive me, I could hardly have been better provided. There were blankets, mattresses, tin basins and jugs (but no water), and various other useful things. The only serious deficiency was in lights—there were only two candles, and no matches. Of the first candle, by now, only a couple of inches was left. Still, I hoped that no more than that would prove necessary. Only, if I let it out, I should have to use up my last match lighting it again. But I decided to risk it, and after making myself an excellent bed on one of the shelves, I turned in, and blew out the light.

After a day so full of excitements and fears, the heavy silence of those cellars might easily have been oppressive, and have banished sleep; but fortunately I am able to sleep in almost any circumstances, and I did not lie awake for many minutes after I lay down. Nevertheless, either the experiences which I had undergone, or the still heavy atmosphere and unaccustomed surroundings must have exerted some influence upon me; for I remember some vivid scenes from a succession of horrid dreams which troubled me, though such dreams come to me very rarely indeed.

In one, I imagined myself to be descending an endless flight of spiral stairs in some old tower, at the bottom of which Mary Cheney was lying in deadly danger, and calling to me. I struggled to reach her, but my limbs refused to be controlled; I reeled and tottered feebly down the narrowest part of the steps, pursued always by some creature of formless horror, with a vulture's head. Again, I was in a dimly-lit room, talking to Forbes, and joking about something, when the smile on his lips changed, in the unaccountable manner of dreams, into a sardonic grin, his face grew long and dark and malignant, and his eyes appeared to me to shine with the very soul of evil.

So great, in fact, was my repulsion and fear of this distorted face that it woke me, and instinctively I put out my hand to switch on the light. Then I remembered where I was, and my senses clearing, I decided to endure the darkness rather than expend my last match for such an absurd reason as a nightmare. I looked at my illuminated watch, and discerned dimly that it was a quarter-to-two. It seemed to me that there was a heavy odour in the place, which had not been noticeable before I went to sleep, and once I thought I heard a slight sound as of a door closing at some distance away; but even as I noticed it, or thought so, I must have fallen asleep again.

When I next woke, I felt very heavy and ill. I looked at my watch, and found it had stopped. It showed ten past

ten. I must have slept the clock round—perhaps more, for
there was no telling how long the watch had stopped. I
longed for water for a good wash, and I would have given
a small fortune for a cup of tea; but as neither of these
was possible I had to content myself with a bottle of white
wine and some biscuits.

I was quite faint before, but these revived me greatly,
and I decided at once to renew my efforts to escape or
make my presence known. I lighted my last candle and
more as a matter of form than with any hope of success I
again tried the door leading out of the first cellar. With
great astonishment, I found it to open as soon as I turned
the handle! Had it simply caught or stuck before, or had
somebody unlocked it? Anyhow, I went through it, and
found myself in another cellar—in fact, a pair of cellars,
exactly like the first pair. Apparently this house was well
provided. It looked as if the cellarage extended the whole
length of it. I went straight through to the opposite door,
and turned the handle. The door was jammed a little, and
I had to exert force to move it; but, as holding my candle
in my left hand I flung it open with my right, I saw standing before me, gazing at the door with terrified eyes—
Mary Cheney.

"Thank God," I exclaimed. "Thank God, I've found you!"

"Why, Mr. Kent," she said, coming forward, "what a
fright you gave me! You really do look a little alarming you
know, with that black face. You oughtn't to call on a lady
like this. Come here and let me make you presentable."

"Oh! bother all that," I said, "Though I must say I'm
glad to find you so cheerful. For heaven's sake tell me what
has happened to you. How do you come to be here?"

"Well, I might say the same to you," she retorted. "But
come and let me put you straight, and I'll tell you all
about it. I can't talk to a man who wears his tie over the
back of his coat!"

16

TRAPPED

The cellar in which we stood was quite luxurious by comparison with my own, for it seemed to have been furnished as a bedroom, and contained a camp bed, with Witney blankets, and the minimum of necessary furniture. But in one important respect it was deficient. No light of any kind had been provided, and the room had been in darkness until I brought in my candle; and as we sat down side by side on the camp bed, Mary Cheney looked about her curiously.

"Whatever is the time?" she asked me.

"Unfortunately, my watch has stopped," I answered. "All I know is that it is after ten."

"Gracious!" she exclaimed. "Then I suppose it's too late to get home to-night. Every one will be in bed."

"To-night?" I repeated. "To-night? Whatever do you mean? Why, it's ten o'clock in the morning, isn't it?"

"In the morning?" she said. "How can it be? I didn't start till after twelve. Besides, it's pitch dark. Mr. Kent, do tell me what has happened! Where are we? Why are you here?"

"Where you are exactly I am afraid I don't know," I said. "But, personally I have been quartered in the wine cellar."

"Well, I must say you look like it," she answered, "But do you mean to say we are in a cellar now?"

129

"I fear so," I replied.

"How on earth did we get down here then? I remember coming into a house because I was feeling faint, and lying down on this bed in an empty room, and that is all."

"I am as bewildered as you are," I said. "Perhaps the best thing will be if you will tell me exactly what happened."

"Very well," she said. "It was all quite simple. Yesterday, Sunday morning . . ."

"Yesterday," I interjected, "was Monday, unless I've gone crazy."

"Well, the day before yesterday then, if you like, I had a telegram from Mr. Forbes, asking me to go over on Monday morning to identify my father's writing. Of course, his cottage is only about twelve miles from us, and the wire said he would send his car for me at twelve o'clock; but I happened to be rather busy that day, so we sent our chauffeur over to see if he wouldn't come to lunch with us instead. However, he wasn't able to, because something or other had cropped up, and he had to alter his plans, and when our man came back just after twelve, he was driving Mr. Forbes's car. He brought a message from Mr. Forbes, apologising and so on, but saying that a matter of urgent importance connected with father's death obliged him to go to Monmouth, and as a good deal might turn on it he would be grateful if I would meet him there. He had sent his own car, he said, for the sake of speed, and would send ours back by his own man, unless we preferred to send over for it.

"It was a little inconvenient, of course, but naturally I was only too anxious to help him in every way, so as soon as I was ready I got into the car and we drove off. You know how cold it was, with that horrid northeast wind, so I had to have the windows up and after we had gone some distance I began to feel very sleepy and faint. Our chauffeur, I must say, was most attentive and nice. He said

perhaps it might be fumes from the engine, so he stopped
the car and put down the windows, and got me some smelling salts. After that I felt better, but I seemed to get more
and more sleepy as we went on; and eventually I dimly
remember his saying that we had arrived, and walking with
great difficulty up a long drive, and lying down on this
bed in a bare room with white walls and a small window.
When I woke up a little while ago I was still lying on
the bed, but it was quite dark, and I began to feel rather
frightened. Then you suddenly burst in at the door—and
that's all I know about it. And I'm dying of curiosity to
know how you came to be here. But still it's rather absurd
to sit here in the cellar. Let's go out and talk about it
upstairs."

"Can you find the way?" I asked, with a momentary
hope which I realised at once was vain.

"I? No, I don't think I can; though I seem to remember
dreaming that I was walking down a spiral staircase somewhere. But surely you can?"

"Curious!" I said. "I dreamed the same thing, only
mine was a nightmare—and a bad one. I am sorry to say I
don't know the way out. We had better go on looking for
it, especially as this is all the candle I have left. Haven't
you any?"

"No—or at least, I couldn't find any in the dark—I
hadn't even any matches."

We searched, but failed to find any more; and it took
very little investigation to assure us that if the spiral staircase of our dreams had any real existence at all it was not
in any part to which we had access; though it might be the
other side of the solid locked door which led out of these
cellars.

We both tried the door in every possible way, but it was
quite immovable, and banging on it produced no answer
but hollow reverberating echoes. We went through the

whole suite of cellars, and I pointed out the shaft by which I had made my accidental entrance, and explained how I also had come to the house in response to a message from Forbes, and must have got into the wrong door by mistake.

"But wherever can we be?" exclaimed Mary. She looked pale and frightened, and my impotence to help in any useful way became still harder to endure.

"I really can't imagine," I answered. "According to the message I had, he ought to be here—somewhere in this house. Forbes seems to have known that you had been brought here, or rather that you were to be brought here, and sent his car on for me so that I could help him to rescue you."

"Rescue me? But why? I only came because he told me to! I don't see how he could know I came here, and if he did, why bring me here, and then have to rescue me? Though I wish he would, I must say. This place is getting on my nerves."

"I am very much afraid the message from him must have been false. Your chauffeur must have misunderstood it, or made it up himself."

"Oh, surely not! The man has seemed perfectly honest. Besides, how did he come to have Mr. Forbes's car?"

"I don't think it was his car," I said. "But certainly the whole thing is quite bewildering. Your chauffeur fetched me from London in Forbes's car— about that there is no doubt—and said that you had gone off at nine o'clock in another car of the same make. Forbes's car was bought at Ringer's in Worcester. . . ."

"So was the one I came in—I noticed it. And I didn't start at nine o'clock. It was after twelve."

"Well, in that case, your chauffeur has been lying. The story he told me was false after all. I thought it might be, when I found myself down here so unexpectedly, but the whole thing beats me completely. I can't imagine how he knew where to find me. Forbes was the only person who knew my London address."

"In that case he must have sent him, surely. And I don't see how our chauffeur could have got Mr. Forbes's car without his consent, though whatever reason Mr. Forbes can have for dumping us down in these horrid cellars and simply leaving us like this, I can't think."

"The possibility is," I said, "that something has happened to Forbes. What do you know about your chauffeur? Because he must have lied, whoever put him up to it."

"Not a great deal. We wanted a man after father's death, and he came to us with an excellent character from some relative of ours, a Mrs. Brook-Sutton."

"Oh! Mrs. Brook-Sutton. Who was it?—oh, yes, Riverton was telling me about her. I shouldn't wonder if your chauffeur may not be as honest as he seems; though I am bound to admit that, if so, he certainly deceived me completely. I hadn't the least doubt of what he told me, until I found myself down here. By the way, this is the last piece of candle I have been able to find, and as neither of us has any matches, I am afraid we are in for rather a gloomy time. If I may suggest it, I think it would be a good plan if you will come into my cellar, and have a meal while we can still see to eat it, and then have another good look round for a way out. What do you say?"

"As a matter of fact, I believe I do want something to eat. I have had nothing but a drink of water. Let's do as you say, and make hay while the sun shines."

We busied ourselves for a few minutes collecting our meal—a simple one of tongue, water biscuits and tinned fruit, with a bottle of Graves, which we set out on top of a dilapidated chest of drawers. Mary was not very expert at drinking out of a bottle, but I was glad to see that the humour of the situation appealed to her, and she laughed quite merrily as she set it down, and I solemnly handed

her a very clumsily cut slab of tongue on a biscuit instead
of a plate.

"You know," she said, "I feel just like those people in
the crypt of old St. Paul's, having a bacchanalian orgy. I
suppose I ought to be frightened, but somehow I am not,
now. It's rather fun to be picnicking down here, and really
I am awfully hungry. Do you mean to tell me it's Tuesday?
Then no wonder I'm hungry, if I haven't had anything
since Monday's breakfast. I can't think how I can have
slept so long as all that. But there's one thing I do hope—
that we get out before the candle is finished. I should hate
being left down here in the dark."

"So should I," I answered, "and we'll have a jolly good
try, but food comes first. You must be simply starving. Try
some of these luscious Californian peaches. You'll have to
eat them with your fingers, but I'll look the other way, if
you like."

"Now, that's very tactless of you. As if I couldn't eat
peaches out of a tin like a real lady. They are no worse
than oranges, anyhow. But it does seem funny to me that
people should leave all these eatables in the cellars. And
this old furniture, too. It's rather lucky for us that they
did, isn't it?"

"It seems more than funny to me," I answered. "It is
beginning to seem amazing. I didn't quite realise it at
first, but it is obvious that some one brought you down
here, and, therefore, the bed and all the rest of it must
have been put here for your benefit. I thought I had tumbled down by accident, but it looks very much now as if
preparations had been made to receive me too. The question is, who on earth can have made them? If it's Forbes,
it certainly seems to me to be a piece of infernal cheek,
and beastly inconsiderate, and I can't imagine what his
object may be. It seems the wildest sort of rot really, but I
might be in some danger from whoever the fellow was that

committed the crime, but where do you come in? What grievance can he have against you? Look here, I can't sit babbling here any longer. It's up to me to get you out of this. Don't you hurry, I will do what I can without moving the candle. And when I get hold of Forbes, I'll wring his neck for putting you in this hole."

"Oh, don't be so hard on him," she said, laughing. "I am sure it's all a mistake of some kind, and probably not his fault at all. Now I've finished, so we can take the light, and have a real good hunt for a way out."

She spoke cheerfully, and showed no signs of fear; but I must admit that, for my part, I felt gloomy and vaguely apprehensive. Who had imprisoned us, and for what end, remained a mystery, however much I puzzled over it; but that he had done it effectively, and that our escape was not going to be simple, my former search had pretty clearly shown. The only possible hope seemed to be the lift-shaft—if it could be dignified by that name—whereby I had entered, but I had already investigated that. However, with Mary's help I dragged the old chest of drawers and set it up on end in the opening, and by climbing on it and holding up the candle, I was able to see the bottom of the lift, on which I had descended, about ten feet above my head. It was covered with a plain sheet of metal, and offered no hold by which it could have been pulled down; and though I again struggled to climb up to it, I met with no better success than the first time; and considering our dwindling candle—which was now scarcely an inch long—I thought it better to desist.

We pulled the chest of drawers away again, and in doing so, chanced to bend slightly one corner of the zinc sheet which covered the floor of the shaft. This revealed that the floor was not continuous with that of the cellar, but separated by a distance of about an eighth of an inch; and on further bending back the zinc along the front edge, we found that the same distance was preserved. It had, therefore, every appearance of being movable. It might merely be the cover of a pit of some sort, or it might, be another lift; and that this was its nature became probable when we discovered that a flange fitted into the slot in the vertical metal rail at each side. I inserted a pencil into this slot, which was about half an inch wide; and found that it encountered no resistance, except when moved sideways. The wall, therefore, was hollow at this point, and perhaps the pulleys which worked the lift were concealed there. Unfortunately this did not help us, for we failed to find them; nor was there any apparent means of handling them, if we succeeded. The momentary hope which our discovery gave us, made it all the harder to bear the futility of it, and Mary's hand trembled a little as she set down the candle, which was already beginning to gutter. The sight stirred me to a kind of frenzy; but in spite of my most strenuous efforts the thing remained obstinately immovable.

"There must surely be some proper way of controlling this lift," said Mary, laying a restraining hand on my shoulder. "Let's see if we can't find a button, or switch, or something. I am sure you can't have to jump on it to make it go."

"But, my dear old friend," I retorted, "where is the electricity to come from? However, we'll look again by all means."

So saying, I picked up what was left of the candle, which immediately collapsed between my finger and thumb, and went out. The darkness swooped down on us, and in the sudden silence that came with it, the ticking of my watch sounded as loud as an alarm clock.

"Oh! I'm most frightfully sorry, Mary," I exclaimed. "What a clumsy fool I am!"

"It doesn't matter a bit, Mr. Kent," she answered. "After all, it would have gone out in another minute anyhow."

"I say!" I expostulated. "You can't go on calling me Mr. Kent at a time like this. Jack would sound much more homely, and I'm in need of some consolation. Besides, what's the good of standing on ceremony in a beastly cellar, when we can't even see each other? Where are you?"

"Here," she said, putting her hand in mine. "But now you'll be angry with me, because I am afraid I must lie down again. I feel half stifled, and my head is swimming. Don't you think the air has got very bad?"

"It's a bit stuffy," I said as lightly as I could, "but you'll soon be all right again."

With my right hand stretched out in front of me, and supporting her with the other, I led her as quickly as the darkness would allow to the bed in the further cellar, and lifted her on to it. The air seemed purer there, and after a minute or two she began to feel better, but I told her to lie still while I went back, determined to find the hidden switch, even in the darkness, if it existed. As I went I noticed a heaviness in the air, like that caused by charcoal burning in a confined space, and in the neighbourhood of the lift it seemed particularly bad. But I could not afford to bother about it, and began exploring the walls and the floor with my hands. My head ached, and a dizzy feeling oppressed me, and when my hand encountered a pair of small bosses on the floor, which felt like large nail-heads, I hardly perceived any significance in the fact, and felt them with vague wonder, which was soon overwhelmed by a horrible feeling of suffocation and faintness. I remember collapsing gradually, in spite of all the resistance I could make, until I lay flat on my face, and then I suppose my senses left me.

17
THE RETICENCE OF MR. FRANCIS

Pursued by a multitude of shadowy monsters on a mountain of precipitous crags, I fled with a struggling heart and limbs of lead. I stumbled over a boulder and fell, and slid towards the precipice, and over it into the abyss. A torrent of falling water caught me, and rolled me over, dashing my head against stones, until I groaned with pain. Then I heard some one saying, a long way off: "He'll do now." I opened my eyes and saw bending over me a vague shape with eyes like moons, which presently resolved itself into an old gentleman wearing spectacles and a skull cap, and beaming at me over his glasses.

A nice, kind old gentleman: but how my head ached. And then, recollection returning, I tried to jump up with the intention of rescuing Mary from some extreme danger, the nature of which I could not yet remember, when a cool hand was laid on my forehead, and I was gently pressed back on to the bed. It was Mary's hand. She was sitting at the bedside, and at sight of her my mind cleared a little more.

"Thank God you are safe," I said. "What happened to me? How did you get away?"

"All in good time, my dear sir," interposed the old gentleman. "All in good time—I want you just to drink this. It will make you feel much better, and clear your

head, and then we will explain. You have had a nasty dose
of carbon monoxide, and you must keep quiet for a while."

He handed me a wine glass full of an amber-coloured
liquid, and watched me approvingly over his spectacles
as I drank it. I returned his gaze. He was a fragile old
man, rather bowed, with white hair and a thin, delicate
face, which inspired confidence. It was a distinguished
and kindly face, if not a strong one. I supposed he was a
doctor, though he looked more like a dean. At any rate,
his medicine, whatever it was, refreshed me wonderfully,
and after a few minutes I was able to sit up and look about
me. I was lying on a sofa, not a bed, as I had supposed,
in a pleasant, airy room with three large windows looking
towards hills: and it was with a delicious sense of relief
that I realised that my imprisonment in the cellar was at
an end.

"No, my dear sir," said the old man, holding up a thin
hand to restrain me as I again tried to rise. "I really must
insist on your lying quiet a little longer. But there is no
reason why you shouldn't hear my part of the story, and
after that I hope you will be well enough to tell me how
this deplorable accident occurred, for I cannot understand
it.

"And first, I suppose you will want to know who I am.
My name is Francis, and Mary here is my niece. Sir William
Cheney was my late wife's brother, and his death has been
a great grief to me. It so happened that I was pottering
about my garden just now, and stooped to pull up a piece
of groundsel, when I noticed fumes coming from a grating in the cellars. Thinking that possibly something had
caught fire, I got the key and went down, which is a thing
I haven't done, I suppose, for six months or more. I took a
candle with me, of course, and I was very much astonished
when I opened the door, to find a bed and furniture in
the cellar, and still more to see a girl sitting on the bed.

When she cried out 'Uncle Frank!' and ran towards me as if she really liked me"—here the old man chuckled—"I wondered if I could believe my eyes. She told me about you, Mr. Kent, and we went to look for you. We found you lying on the floor unconscious. I thank God that I was led to pick that piece of groundsel; for, if you had lain there another five minutes, my dear boy, I fear it might have been too late. We got you up here—Mary brought you up and I helped her, that's the truth of it—and so here you are. Now there's been no time as yet for me to hear how you both came to be in the cellars under my house, and if you feel well enough to tell me . . ."

"Certainly I do," I answered. "But I hoped you were going to tell us. We are both rather bewildered about it."

"Indeed!" said Mr. Francis, "do you mean that you didn't come here of your own volition?"

"Well, it would not be quite true to say that. By the way, what time is it?"

"It's nearly five. And that reminds me. We will ring for Mrs. Hughes and get her to bring us some tea. No doubt you will both be ready for a cup after your visit to the cellars. How long were you down there?"

"That depends on what day it is now," said Mary. "It was Monday morning when I was brought into this house."

"Monday morning!" exclaimed the old man, with a look of deep anxiety, or even fear. "My dear child! But this is Tuesday evening!" He took her hand between his own. "Tell me, my dear," he said, "how all this happened. Believe me, I am truly sorry that it should have happened in my house, however it came about, and if I hadn't been away for the week-end. . . . But there! Let me hear your story."

Mary explained how Forbes had sent his car for her with a message requesting her to meet him in Monmouth, and how she had been taken ill on the way, and came in to rest, and later had woken up to find herself in the cellar.

"And who may this Mr. Forbes be, my dear?" asked Mr. Francis, when she had finished. "He was not one of your father's friends, I think?"

"Perhaps I had better explain about that," I said, "as I was responsible for introducing him. He was staying at the 'White Hart' at Luttercombe, where I was also, and he became interested in Professor Cheney's death, and found circumstances which pointed to"—I was going to say murder, but thought better of it—"to some mystery in connection with it, and asked me to join him in investigating the matter. Lady Cheney had heard of him through Dr. Armstrong and was anxious to see him, so we went up to Cheney Park together. That is how he became acquainted with Miss Cheney."

Mr. Francis had been looking apprehensive, but what I said seemed to relieve his anxiety, although he still seemed deeply concerned. At this point, Mrs. Hughes, who proved to be the old lady whom Forbes and I had interviewed at the "witch's cottage," brought in the tea, and Mr. Francis courteously asked Mary to pour out for us.

"I gather, therefore," he then said, turning to me, "that you knew nothing of Mr. Forbes before? But no doubt he was the kind of man who inspires confidence. He showed you some credentials, perhaps?"

"Well, no; and I asked for none, but he told me something of his history. Of course I was a little doubtful of him at first, but our association did inspire me with confidence in him, and, moreover, I formed a high opinion of his abilities."

"Quite so; a very natural result. Well, then, how did you yourself come to be in the situation in which I found you?"

"Well, the explanation is this. Forbes wished me to go to London in connection with the case, and on Monday morning I had a letter from him suggesting that I might stay there a day or two longer. But on that afternoon I found Forbes's car waiting for me, with Lady Cheney's chauffeur, who said that he brought a message from Forbes. The message was, briefly, that Miss Cheney had been kidnapped, and that I was to return in the car and meet Forbes here. I was to enter by the side door, and wait in the first room on the right of the passage—at least that is how I understood it. I have since thought that perhaps it was the room on the left which was intended."

"The room on the left? That would be—let me see—yes, that would be the back entrance to the pantry. I can scarcely think Mr. Forbes would want to meet you in the pantry, unless, of course, he was after the spoons. The door opposite, if I recollect rightly, is a cupboard, isn't it?"

"A curious sort of cupboard," I replied. "As soon as I stepped into it, it descended, landed me in the cellar, and left me there."

"Is that really a fact, Mr. Kent? You astound me. I had no idea there was any such dangerous thing in the house. You see, this is a large place for an old man like me. I use two or three rooms, and I very seldom stray outside them. I doubt if I have been in that part of the house ever since I have been here, although I looked round it all when I first came in. My recollection was that it was a cupboard opposite the pantry, but I have never, I think, examined it. It seems to me exceedingly odd of Mr. Forbes to ask you to meet him in such a place, especially in view of the result. What is your own impression of the matter?"

"It has puzzled us extremely. The most natural and obvious supposition would be that both messages were false, devised by some person who wished—we can't imagine why—to get us out of the way: but the obstacle is that no one but Forbes knew where to find me in London."

"And it was his car, I think you said, which fetched you both? I hesitate to cast any doubt on the character of a man whom you have seen, and I haven't; but, as an old man with a long and sometime sad experience behind me, I may not offend you if I say that an outsider would think you had accepted Mr. Forbes rather too easily. Has he had any opportunity of learning the arrangement of this house?"

"Why, yes, I must admit he has," I answered, rather reluctantly. "In fact, I had better make a clean breast of it, and tell you that we both tried to investigate this house, and Forbes, I believe, afterwards did so—or at least, I know that was his intention, but on the occasion to which I refer, we got no further than the Lodge. The man there, your chauffeur, as he described himself, told us that he had strict orders to admit no strangers."

"He was quite right. I have been strict with him about that. I accepted the offer of this house a year or two ago from—from an acquaintance, because it is away in the wilds, and I wanted peace and quiet. My life, as I hinted just now, has had its troubles, and one gets tired. I am contented now to live alone here, and potter round my garden, and look after my pigeons. They don't play you false, or try to get the better of you; and if an old man gives his heart to them, it may be foolish of him, but he need not be afraid that they will break it. But I am sorry you should have been turned away, Kent. Any friend of Mary's would have been welcome, if I had known of it."

"It is curious that you should mention your pigeons," I said, "for the fact is it was in connection with some pigeons that Forbes wished to see you."

"What was it that he wanted to know?" he asked. "I pride myself on being able to answer most questions about them."

"In this case," I said, "he wanted to know the destination of a basket of pigeons which were adorned with a black mitre and were brought, we thought, to this house."

It was not without reflection that I had shown our hand to this extent. I found it hard to believe that the frail, kindly old gentleman who sat beside me was a criminal, or engaged in any criminal conspiracy, and I thought I should risk a little, and might get some light on a mystery which seemed so far merely to grow darker. But there was a noticeable embarrassment in the manner of his reply— or so it seemed to me, though Mary afterwards disagreed. She would not admit that he would stoop to any kind of concealment, or be concerned in anything shady, any more than her father would have done. After all, he had been her favourite when she was a little girl, and he used to play with her, on the rare occasions when he visited Cheney Park in the old days, so her feeling was natural enough. The substance of his answer was that he was constantly sending birds all over the country, but could recollect none which were decorated with a mitre. He then changed the subject and began talking about the origin of the fumes from which we had suffered in the cellars.

"You must know," he said, "that there is a derelict mine quite close to this house—you noticed it, perhaps?— and I have heard it said, though I don't know with what authority or truth, that some of the workings are under our foundations. I can only suppose that some gases were generated underground, and managed to find their way into the cellars. It is the first time that I have ever noticed such a thing, and I must have it seen to. I have no knowledge of mines, and very little of gases, but I suppose such a thing could occur. You should know, Mary, as your father's daughter. What do you say?"

"I should think it's quite possible, Uncle Frank," she answered. "But it's strange that it came so suddenly, just as our light went out. It almost seemed as if some one was lying in wait for us. However, all's well that ends well, isn't it?"

"I am not so sure, my dear," he answered. "After this you had better be on your guard. I should make some more inquiries about Mr. Forbes, Kent, if I were in your place. And what about your chauffeur, Mary, who brought the message for him? Are you sure of him?"

"We certainly thought so," she answered. "We have always found him thoroughly satisfactory, and he came to us with an excellent character from a Mrs. Brook-Sutton."

At the mention of this name, a most startling change came over Mr. Francis. He grew very pale, and half rose from his chair, and then sank down again with a kind of sob.

Mary was immediately at his side. "You are ill, Uncle dear," she said. "What is it? What is the matter?"

"No, no, my dear," he answered brokenly. "It is nothing—nothing. I hope the danger is over now. No, don't alarm yourself, my dear. It was just a little faintness, and you see, I have recovered already. But perhaps I had better rest a little. Now, will you stay here to-night, or do you feel that you ought to get back to your mother?"

"If you are sure you will be all right, Uncle Frank," she answered, "I think I ought to get back. Mother, I expect, will be getting very anxious about me."

"I think that is the right thing to do," he answered. "Very well, then, I will order the car for you, and Mr. Kent perhaps will see you safely home, if he is going back to Luttercombe?"

I replied that I would do so with the greatest pleasure, and a few minutes later the car was at the door. It was the same limousine which Forbes and I had tracked from Wilmer Deeping and was driven by the same young chauffeur.

"You must have a good rest to-night, both of you," said Mr. Francis, "after your painful experience to-day. The adjourned inquest is to-morrow, I believe, and I expect you will both have to appear. I hope it won't be a very painful ordeal for you. Good-bye, and good fortune to you. Come and see me again, when all these troubles are cleared away."

Mary was silent as we drove back; and I was no more talkative, for I was deeply interested in considering the case of Mr. Francis. Freed from the fascination of his white hair, his frail figure, his kindly face, his gentle and courteous manner, I found myself more and more convinced of his complicity. Surely of no one could it ever be more aptly said that "he smiled, and smiled, and was a villain." The evidence against him, as I reflected upon it, seemed to me overwhelming and conclusive.

That he was in constant touch with Shortditch—another loathsome hypocrite—might be said really to be common knowledge. The car drove to and fro between the two houses so frequently that it was familiar to the garage hands of Wilmer Deeping. We had, with our own eyes, seen it convey almost to Francis's door those pigeons with the black mitre. And Forbes's conviction that those pigeons were taken to him in exchange for his own, wearing a black crown, seemed to me unassailable. He was the leader of the whole gang, if the black crown was his symbol. But apart from that, what explanation or excuse could be given for the outrageous treatment of Mary and myself? None whatever! He was contented politely to explain that he was unaware that there was a death-trap in his house; he was unaware that his cellars had been furnished and stored with food; he had no connection at all with the whole thing except that by Divine guidance he was led to pull up a bit of groundsel! Certainly he and Shortditch were a fine pair! And not content with this sickening piece of hypocrisy, he had cunningly used every possible occasion to insinuate suspicion against Forbes, even to the extent of suggesting that Forbes was a common thief, after the pantry spoons! And that Forbes knew of the trap, and, I suppose, furnished the cellars!

And again, what sinister connection existed between Mr. Francis and Mrs. Brook-Sutton? If ever I have seen consciousness of some guilty secret, it was shown by Francis, at the mention of her name. Nevertheless, my indignation and my conviction were alike unprofitable in the absence of Forbes. Until I rejoined him, I must possess my soul in patience, for nothing could be done.

18

The Caped Coat

When at last I re-entered the "White Hart" at Luttercombe after what seemed to me a long interval of time, although it was less than a week in reality, I found, as Mr. Francis had surmised, that I was subpoenaed for the adjourned inquest. It was to be held at 11 a.m. in the village hall, and the language in which I was commanded to attend it was compelling rather than polite. Forbes had not been seen at the "White Hart," as I learnt from the voluble Mrs. Huggins, since the day when we had left it together, carrying the Gladstone bag; and a prepaid reply telegram to his Worcestershire address brought me no answer. It was, therefore, with great uneasiness that I awaited the inquest; but I had no suspicion of what the evidence was actually to reveal.

The village hall was only a few minutes' walk distant, and having nothing to distract my thoughts, I became so impatient that, in the end, I set out at least a quarter of an hour too early. The hall was a commonplace brick and slate building, containing two rooms, joined by a communicating door. The constable directed me into the larger of these two rooms. On the left, as I entered, was a large table for the coroner and his assistants; and the remaining three sides were lined with benches.

Some of those nearest the coroner's table were reserved for witnesses and for the jury, the jury being to the right of the table, and the witnesses on the left. The latter benches, when I entered, were occupied only by Mary and her mother, who I supposed had suffered the same uneasy feeling as myself, and a young, inconspicuous-looking clergyman who sat on the extreme end of the bench, and seemed therefore to be of a retiring and inoffensive disposition. I walked across the room and greeted Lady Cheney and Mary, and took my place beside them. The body of the room was sprinkled with people, and more came in by twos and threes, until it was pretty well filled. Most of them I had seen about the village, but some were strange to me. I was surprised, and rather amused, to see Mrs. Huggins enter in company with the village policeman, and sit down with him on the bench behind our own. They were followed a little later by a dark, sedate man of middle age, quietly dressed and clean-shaven, who sat next them.

None of us were in a mood for conversation, and even Mrs. Huggins had nothing to say. For my own part, I was occupied in trying to conjecture what evidence I was expected to be able to give, and why my presence was required; but more for the sake of politeness than from a desire for information, I asked Lady Cheney about the coroner, and whether he was formidable.

I learned that he was a Mr. Drummond-Cavendish, who had lately been a friend of Professor Cheney. He was a well-known man who, to the astonishment of his friends, had suddenly, some few years before this time, abandoned a promising political career and retired to his place at Norton Cheney, where he devoted himself to country pursuits, and dabbled in science and philosophy. What concerned me more was that his manner was described as rather overbearing.

At a minute or two before eleven o'clock, the jury filed in, having apparently assembled in the other room, and took their seats, rather sheepishly, opposite our own. They were soon followed by an inspector of police and others, with the coroner himself, who seated themselves at the table. The appearance of Mr. Drummond-Cavendish was not one which would reassure the evil-doer. He looked to me more fitted for a major-general than a philosopher, having a hard-bitten, weather-beaten sort of face, with an iron-grey clipped moustache of the military fashion, mottled complexion, and hard eyes.

After the jury had been sworn, he inquired, in a voice suggestive of the parade ground, whether all the witnesses who had been subpoenaed were present.

He was informed that Mr. Alfred Thomas and Mr. Horton Forbes were not.

"I shall begin the inquiry without them," he said. "If witnesses do not attend punctually, they have themselves to thank for whatever penalty may be imposed."

A brief silence followed this pronouncement, during which the coroner put on a pair of glasses, and looked over the papers which lay before him on a sheet of pink blotting-paper. Then he looked up.

"You are aware, gentlemen," he said, addressing the jury, "that the business of this court to-day is to continue our inquiry as to when, where, and by what means, Professor Cheney met his death. While the inquest has stood adjourned, certain new evidence has come to light, which will be put before you. It will be your duty to consider it attentively, without letting yourselves be influenced by any preconceived opinions, and to give a true verdict in accordance with the evidence. Before we proceed, my duty is to read to you depositions taken in this court last week."

The substance of these was that Professor Cheney had died from heart failure, following an injection of morphine, before 3 o'clock on the morning of March 12th, but that there was nothing to show by whom this injection was made.

"Our object now, therefore," continued the coroner, "is to discover whether the injection was made, accidentally or otherwise, by the Professor himself, or whether circumstances point to its being administered by some other person. Call the Reverend Frederick Pennefather."

This witness proved to be the shy young clergyman, who stood up and took the oath in a manner indicative of extreme nervousness, while Mr. Drummond-Cavendish regarded him grimly.

"Will you tell the court, Mr. Pennefather, who you are, and what you know about this matter?"

"I am the vicar of St. Luke's, Hilton," said the clergyman, speaking in an indistinct, hurried manner, "and on the night of the eleventh . . ."

"One moment, Mr. Pennefather. Kindly speak as slowly and distinctly as you can, as your evidence has to be recorded. Where is Hilton?"

"Hilton is a village about ten miles from here—in a northwesterly direction."

The coroner nodded, and the witness resumed:

"On the night of the eleventh, shortly after 2 a.m., that is, on the morning of the twelfth—I was summoned to the deathbed of an old lady, one of my parishioners. I remained with her for the greater part of an hour, and she passed away at ten minutes to three. I then left the house. When I reached the cross-roads, outside the village on my way home, I met a car driving slowly. It was coming from the direction of Kington, and it took the road to Luttercombe; and as it turned I saw clearly by the moonlight the face of one of the occupants, and recognised Professor

Cheney, whom I know well by sight. He was sitting on the left of the car, and seemed to be asleep. I could not see the face of the driver."

"Can you describe the dress of either of the occupants?"

"Professor Cheney seemed to be wearing a dark cap and a dark jacket. He had no overcoat. The other had a dark hat which threw his face in shadow, and a dark, caped coat."

"How was it that you took no steps to give these facts in evidence last week?"

"I had to go away next day to take a retreat in the north of England, and was unaware of the Professor's death until I returned, when I told the police."

"Is it your habit to attend parishioners who die in the small hours of the morning?"

"Yes, sir, if I am sent for. I regret that I am not sent for more often."

"Very proper, of course—most conscientious. Now, are you prepared to assert that the deceased was still alive when you saw him?"

"No, I think he was already dead, but it is impossible to be certain."

"Considering the dimness of moonlight, how could you be sure that the driver was wearing a caped coat?"

"Because his hands being on the wheel the cape was drawn away from the body of the coat. It partly covered his arms and was easily distinguished."

"Thank you, Mr. Pennefather, that will do."

With suitable expression of his own sympathy, and that of the court, the coroner then called upon Lady Cheney. His first inquiry concerned the missing witness, Alfred Thomas.

"I understand, Lady Cheney," he said, "that this man Alfred Thomas is in your employment. Can you tell us where he is? I am told that his evidence is of some importance."

"I am sorry I can't," she replied. "He seems to have disappeared. We haven't seen him since Sunday. On that day my daughter had a telegram from Mr. Forbes asking her to go over the following morning to identify her father's handwriting. It was a little inconvenient, and we sent our chauffeur, Thomas, at his own suggestion, to ask Mr. Forbes to lunch with us instead. He returned later, in Mr. Forbes's car, and said that Mr. Forbes was obliged to go to Monmouth, and urgently wished my daughter to go in the car he had sent and meet him there. She did so; but on the way she was taken ill—it almost seems as if she was drugged by some one—for she woke up to find herself shut in a cellar; and there, poor girl, she had to stay until the next evening, when she was rescued by Mr. Francis, who occupies the house. She tells me that Thomas was civil and attentive to her when she felt faint, but, anyhow, we have not seen him since."

"That is certainly very strange," he said. "Especially since Mr. Forbes is also absent. What of Thomas's character? Is he a trustworthy man in your opinion?"

"Quite, so far as we know," she answered, "but he had not been very long with us."

"Well," he said, "perhaps we shall learn whether his absence is voluntary, or whether, as happened to your daughter, with whom we all sympathise, he is detained against his will. Now I want to ask you—did Sir William ever himself use drugs? Is it likely that he would have taken this injection of morphine for any purpose of his own accord?"

"I feel sure he would not. He never used any drugs. He had a horror of them."

"Thank you. Then you think that this poison must have been given by some one else—whether accidentally or otherwise?"

"I do."

"Can you suggest any motive which could lead any one to such an act?"

"No; I know of none at all."

Mary Cheney was then sworn, and was asked the same questions. She was evidently reluctant to answer, and hesitated.

"Come, Miss Cheney," said the coroner, in a deliberately gentle voice. "The point is very important, and if you know of anything which might possibly throw light on such a motive you ought to tell us."

"I hesitated," she said, "because I promised my father to tell nobody. Will it do if I say that I know my father had discovered a dangerous scientific secret?"

"That will be quite sufficient. We need not inquire into the actual nature of the secret; but I understand you to mean that it would have a negotiable value?"

"Yes; it certainly would."

"Until this moment, was any one aware existence of this secret, except yourself?"

"Nobody, except"—here she blushed a little—"except Mr. Kent and Mr. Forbes. I told Mr. Kent after my father's death, so that he and Mr. Forbes might help us."

"It would have been better, I think, to confide in the police. Is this secret in your possession?"

"No; but I gathered that Mr. Forbes had recovered it. I supposed it to be the paper which he wanted me to identify."

"What is your meaning?" the coroner asked, amid an expectant hush, "when you say Mr. Forbes 'recovered' it? From whom do you suppose he recovered it?"

"I suppose," she said doubtfully, "from the—the murderer."

"Who led you to suppose that?"

"Mr. Kent."

"Indeed! Well, thank you, Miss Cheney. I will hear what Mr. Kent can tell us."

At last my turn had come. In some vague way, I felt that the coroner was suspicious of me, if not hostile. I could not quite see where the evidence was tending, but somehow I felt uneasy.

"Miss Cheney has told us," he began, in a harder voice, "that you, Mr. Kent, led her to suppose that Mr. Forbes had 'recovered' possession of a valuable secret and, if so, is presumably still in possession of it. On what grounds did you say that?"

"I said it," I replied, "because on Monday morning last I received a letter from Forbes saying that he had just received the formula in what he believed to be the Professor's writing; and because Lady Cheney's chauffeur showed me a telegram sent on Sunday to Miss Cheney asking her to come and identify this writing."

"Have you the letter which you say you received?"

"No; I left it at my hotel in London."

"Did the letter explain in what manner Mr. Forbes 'received' this formula?"

"Yes; he said a bird brought it."

At this there was an audible titter, immediately suppressed, as the coroner glared round. To my surprise, he made no comment on my badly expressed answer, and did not pursue the matter.

"Why did Lady Cheney's chauffeur—by whom I suppose you mean the man Alfred Thomas—come to see you, and where?"

"At the Lincoln Hotel, Berners Street. He came with a message, which I now believe to be quite false, which he alleged came from Mr. Forbes."

"Never mind your beliefs, sir; kindly give us the facts!"

"Alfred Thomas came with Forbes's car. The message, said to be from Mr. Forbes, was that Miss Cheney had been abducted, and that I was to come down in the car and help Forbes find her."

"Well, what resulted?"

"I went to the appointed place. The room in which I was to meet Forbes proved to be a kind of lift, and before I knew where I was, I was deposited in the cellars."

"Were those the same cellars in which Miss Cheney was confined?"

"Yes; the same set of cellars, but at first we were separated by a closed door."

"How long did you remain there?"

"Just under twenty-four hours."

"You were unable to get out?"

"Quite unable. The outer doors were locked, and we could find no means of working the lift."

"How did you get out eventually? Did Mr. Forbes come to the rescue?"

"No; we were rescued by Mr. Francis."

"Very well. Now, I understand that you first brought Mr. Forbes into this case. Do you know anything of his antecedents?"

I mentioned what I knew, which seemed very little, and added that he was well known to Superintendent Channing of Scotland Yard.

Mr. Drummond-Cavendish merely smiled rather grimly, and shook his head. This concluded my evidence.

"Let us turn to another aspect of the case," said the coroner. "Mr. Pennefather has told us that the car was driven by a man wearing a dark hat and caped coat. Has any one any information which may bear on that man's identity?"

The constable stolidly rose, and deposed that at 6.05 a.m. on March 12th he met a man, dressed as described, and carrying a small black bag, at about two and a half miles from the village of Luttercombe, in a lane which runs round the outside of Cheney Park. The man was walking at a good pace towards the village, and said "Good morning" to the constable as he passed. Questioned, he said that there was a back way into Cheney Park through the woods, about half a mile farther down the lane, which led, by a roundabout way, to Norton Cheney.

Next, Mrs. Huggins stated that Mr. Horton Forbes had engaged a room on the afternoon of March 8th. He had often been out most of the day, but only once at night. That was on the night of the 11th, when his bed was unused. She had let him in at a quarter to seven next morning. He was then wearing a dark hat, dark caped coat, and was carrying a small black bag.

I listened to this evidence with bewilderment. Surely it could not be supposed that Forbes himself was guilty of the crime? But I had little time for reflection; for the coroner at once proceeded to call Albert Dean.

"You are, I believe," he said, "employed as a manservant by Mr. Horton Forbes. Can you give us any information as to his movements on the night of March 11th?"

"No, sir," he answered. "I was not with Mr. Forbes at that time. He wished me to remain in Worcestershire. The address which he gave me for letters was the 'White Hart,' Luttercombe."

"When did you see him last?"

"Last Monday morning, sir. Mr. Forbes on that day received a visit from a young man whom I understood to be employed by Lady Cheney. A few minutes later he handed me a small parcel to deposit at his bank, and then hurried into the car and drove off with the young man."

"Do you know where he is now?"

"I think so, sir. On Monday evening I received a telegram from him at Southampton . . ."

"Is this the telegram?" asked the coroner, exhibiting it. The witness assented, and the coroner then read it out, and passed it to the jury. It read: "Southampton Docks, 7.45 p.m. Forward letters Poste Restante, Le Havre, Seine Inférieure, France. Forbes."

I was thunderstruck at this piece of news. Lady Cheney and Mary seemed equally amazed.

"Did you feel any doubt as to the authenticity of this telegram?" the coroner inquired.

The witness replied that he did not.

"Have you acted upon it?"

"Yes; I forwarded some letters the same evening, and also requested Mr. Forbes to send me a ring of keys which I required."

"Have you received any reply?"

"I received the keys this morning, sir," replied the witness.

"Thank you," said the coroner. "This is decisive."

And looking over his notes reflectively, he prepared to sum up the case.

19

INTERVENTION OF MR. DEAN

Presently the coroner put down his papers and took off his glasses, which he held in his hand. As he spoke he emphasised his points by tapping them on the table.

"Members of the Jury," he began, "I have no doubt that you have followed the evidence attentively, and, if so, you cannot have failed to appreciate the importance of the facts which have been put before you, or to see that they put an entirely new complexion on a case which looked, at first sight, like one of death from natural causes, or at most from accident. But the evidence which we have heard this morning points strongly, I think I may say, conclusively, to wilful murder. Let me remind you what the facts are.

"We have learnt, first, that the deceased was not alone in his car on that terrible night; nor was he driving it himself. On the contrary, he was being driven in the dead of night, at three in the morning, by a person described as wearing a dark hat and caped coat. The deceased himself was in an attitude which, to the witness, suggested sleep; but there can be little doubt, gentlemen, that he was already dead. He had been dead, according to medical evidence, for over four hours at 7 a.m., and so his death must have occurred within a short time before this, perhaps within a few minutes. But what action did the man driving the car take? Might he not have been expected to stop at this village, which he passed so near, and get medical assistance, or at least to report the death to the proper quarters? He did no such thing. He went calmly on, and took the road to Luttercombe.

"When we next hear of this car, at 6 a.m., it is standing in Cheney avenue, with the deceased's body arranged behind the wheel, as if he had been driving it; and so cunningly had this atrocious crime been planned that even the doctor who examined the body was disposed to attribute his death to simple failure of the heart. But for the conscientiousness of Mr. Pennefather in visiting his flock, the vital fact that there had been another man in the car might never have come to light, and murder might never have been suspected.

"The man in the dark hat and coat vanished from the scene, and we lose trace of him. But, strangely enough, that same morning, we hear of two other men wearing a similar costume. One is walking at 6 a.m. away from a back entrance to Cheney Park in the direction of Luttercombe; the other arrives at Luttercombe at a quarter to seven, where he is known as Mr. Horton Forbes. No one, I imagine, will entertain any doubt that the last two men were really one man. The additional detail of the black bag seems decisive as to that, when we consider that the number of individuals in or near this village who dress in the manner described is very small indeed.

"We may take it, then, that it was this Mr. Forbes who was walking down that lane at 6 a.m. Whether he was also the man who wore a similar costume in the car it is for you to consider. If not, it is highly unfortunate that he has chosen this moment to go to France. He could have explained to us where he had been all night, and why he was in the neighbourhood of the crime at an early hour of the morning. As it is, we must form our own opinion.

"We next learn that the deceased, who was a distinguished man of science, had discovered some secret which, we are assured, would be of negotiable value—possibly very great value; and further, that the existence of this secret was known only to three persons, Miss Cheney, Mr. Kent, and Mr. Forbes. We learn that on Monday, the day after Mr. Pennefather had given his highly important information to the police, a number of very strange events begin to occur. Two of the participators in the secret are, it seems, unfortunate. Mr. Forbes's car calls for Miss Cheney; Mr. Forbes's car calls for Mr. Kent; both these young people, unsuspiciously, out of the kindness of their hearts, act upon a message which they receive from Mr. Forbes, and, as a result, find themselves immured for the best part of two days in some cellars, where they are at last accidentally discovered by a gentleman named" (here he referred to his notes) "named Mr. Francis.

"What can be the explanation of this? The explanation, gentlemen, appears not very far to seek when we learn that Mr. Forbes is also, in all probability, in possession of the precious formula himself. A man of criminal tendencies would be likely enough to see that the best way to secure possession of it would be to dispose, for the time being, of the only other two persons who might know that he possessed it, in such a way that he would be free to make his escape to some foreign land, and disappear before he could be traced. I will go further, and say that such a man might have been even better pleased if Miss Cheney and Mr. Kent had never again seen the light. We do not know that Mr. Forbes was such a man; we know very little indeed of Mr. Forbes; there is, unfortunately, no one here who can vouch for him. . . ."

Here the police-inspector whispered to the coroner for a few moments. It struck me that he did not altogether feel at ease.

"Inspector Trench reminds me," the coroner resumed, "that Mr. Forbes enjoys the confidence of certain highly placed and trustworthy people, whose names he has mentioned to me. I am glad to give the greatest possible weight to this fact. But nevertheless, it does happen sometimes that confidence is abused, and that on an exceptional temptation a man of excellent antecedents will stoop to crime. You must bear both these facts in mind, but you will have to give your verdict solely on the evidence before you.

"What it amounts to is this: that Mr. Forbes came to Luttercombe shortly before the commission of the murder, for no apparent reason if he was, as he pretended, an insurance agent. This is not a good centre for such an occupation, and no one has come forward to say that he transacted any business in this neighbourhood. On the night of the crime, his bed was unused. He was out all night. But we have unimpeachable evidence that early next morning he was returning to this village by a road which actually leads from a back entrance to Cheney Park, about half an hour after the body of the deceased was discovered: and that he was dressed in the same unusual costume as the man who was seen driving the car at 3 a.m. Moreover, as we have learnt from Mr. Kent, he had studied medicine; he would have the requisite knowledge for giving the injection of morphine and for knowing what would be a fatal dose. This, certainly, is merely circumstantial evidence, but when we ask for what motive the crime was committed, we find him more directly incriminated. Only one motive had been suggested, and it is a sufficient one—the acquirement of a valuable secret. The evidence is that Forbes is in possession of that secret, and we find, further, that as soon as information pointing to murder was in the hands of the police, Mr. Forbes ingeniously arranged the disappearance of the only two persons, beside himself, who knew that secret, or in fact that it existed at all. Meanwhile, although he has been deeply concerned in this case, as even his friends testify, he has very quietly left the country—presumably taking the secret with him—without a word to any one. If you think, as I do, that there is a *prima facie* case against him, I shall commit him to take his trial at the next Assizes."

It was impossible for me to sit quietly by without saying something in my friend's defence, and I therefore interposed, and explained how Forbes had found the broken piece of needle in the carburetor, and that it was owing to this that Dr. Armstrong had discovered the fact that an injection had been given. That, I argued, conclusively showed that Forbes was not guilty; otherwise, instead of showing me this piece of needle, he would certainly have hidden it.

"You said, I think," he remarked, "that you interrupted Forbes—came upon him at work?"

I admitted that.

"Then," said he, "there is an alternative explanation. He was bound to give you some very convincing reason for his extraordinary conduct in tampering with the carburetor of a car from which a dead body had just been removed. It was in itself an act likely to arouse instantaneous suspicion. He bluffed you by telling the truth; and most probably diverted your suspicion to some one else by that very act."

Here one of the jurymen asked me why, on my view, Mr. Forbes had been led to examine the carburetor? Could I suggest any reason, except that he knew it contained a damning piece of evidence which he wished to remove?

I explained the reasoning which Forbes had put before me in the train, but I felt that I did not carry my hearers with me. Either I failed to put it clearly, or it was too subtle for their understanding, and I realised with dismay that the jury regarded what I had said as telling against Forbes instead of in his favour. Feeling that to say more would only make things worse I sat down.

The coroner was about to resume his direction of the jury, when another interruption came, from an unexpected quarter.

Prefacing his remarks with a discreet cough, Mr. Albert Dean rose and said that, seeing how things were going, he wished to be allowed to give the name of the gentleman who interviewed the Rev. Fielding Shortditch at the Old Mill, Wilmer Deeping, at 3 p.m. on the afternoon of Monday last.

The coroner glared at Dean. He was plainly very much annoyed.

"That is perfectly irrelevant," he said. "Mr. Shortditch's name has never been mentioned in connection with this matter, and any one who saw him on Monday cannot possibly have any bearing on the case. Let us have no more of these frivolous interruptions."

Inspector Trench, however, thought otherwise. I noticed that he started when Dean made his request, and now he turned to the coroner. What he said was audible to me, though probably not to the court at large. It was that the police had a complete record of the conversation referred to, which had been taken by dictaphone, and which furnished clear evidence against the speakers, but by a blunder, or misfortune, their representative could not prove the identity of either party to it.

This being explained, the coroner asked Dean how he came to be present, and whether he could swear to the identity of either or both of the parties. Dean replied that he could swear to both, that he went to the Old Mill for that purpose on instructions given him by Mr. Forbes, just before he left in his car on Monday morning. Mr. Forbes had said that he had information that the Rev. Shortditch

was expecting a visitor at that time and place, and requested Dean to go and find out who it was, and, if possible,
overhear what was said. Mr. Forbes added that he had also
wired Scotland Yard, but that they might not respond.
Dean went as directed, and saw both parties clearly, but
could only have overheard by entering the premises, which
it was not his place to do.

The moment Dean had finished his statement, the coroner anticipated some further questions which the Inspector was about to ask, by suggesting that as it was already
past one, and the hearing of this new evidence was likely
to prolong the case considerably, they should adjourn for
an hour for luncheon, and resume at 2.30. No objection
was offered to this course, and the court rose.

As the coroner moved towards the door leading into the
other room, it suddenly opened, and there, to the amaze-
ment of us all, stood Horton Forbes, caped coat and all
complete. On Mr. Drummond-Cavendish the effect of this
apparition was even more startling; for a moment or two
he stood gazing at Forbes as if he were some horrible spec-
tre, and then, with a kind of gasp, he collapsed on the
floor. I supposed that he had fainted, but learnt afterwards
that he had suffered a stroke of apoplexy. In any case, it
was obvious to every one that the unexpected and dramatic appearance of Forbes had given him an unaccountably
severe shock. Struck by a sudden thought, I turned and
whispered to Dean, who stood near me:

"Who was the gentleman whose name you were going
to mention just now in connection with Mr. Shortditch?"

"It was Mr. Cavendish himself, sir," replied Dean.

20

A Luncheon Party

Dean's statement was certainly startling, and it explained much which had puzzled me. Throughout the hearing, I had felt that everything was being made to tell against Forbes, and yet I had not been able to detect any wilful perversion of the facts, or actual suppression of evidence in his favour. Although I had thought the coroner biased, his bias had not seemed unjustifiable having regard to the evidence submitted to him.

But now it seemed that he himself was in the conspiracy, and it was a plausible supposition that he had skilfully elicited just such evidence as he wished, and no other, with the deliberate intention of bringing in a verdict against Forbes, so that on his return from France he would be at once arrested, and unable to interfere again in the conspirators' schemes for some time. I wondered what had brought Forbes back so suddenly, as much as I still wondered why he had ever gone; but his re-appearance had certainly been dramatic. It was unfortunate that the jury were left at the moment with an impression that he was guilty of murder, but I felt sure that it would not be long before Dean's information became public property, and eventually, I supposed, the entire proceedings at this inquest would be annulled.

After some minutes, during which we were hesitating what to do, Dr. Armstrong came in and announced, informally, that the coroner was too ill to resume the hearing, and suggested that any one who had business elsewhere would be well advised to get on with it. Forbes, in the meantime, was deep in conversation with the two representatives of Scotland Yard. Most of the people went out in a body; a few lingered, in hope, perhaps, of further excitement, but they also gradually melted away, until at last there was no one left but myself, the Cheneys, and Mr. Albert Dean. At this point Forbes, who was standing with his back to us in the doorway between the two rooms, talking to the police, happened to turn round and caught sight of us. He immediately broke off his conversation and came over.

"Lady Cheney and Miss Cheney," he said, as he shook hands with them, "I owe you both a thousand apologies. I have just learnt with infinite regret that you, Miss Cheney, were, after all, subjected to most outrageous treatment by these ruffians. It was a contingency which I ruled out, in this case, as being entirely outside probability, but I was wrong, and I take very great blame to myself that it should have happened. I beg you to forgive me. I am at least glad to see that you are looking none the worse for your unpleasant adventure."

Mary gave him a friendly smile without any hint of resentment in it. I think she felt none—no more than I did myself.

"That's quite all right, Mr. Forbes," she said. "I felt all along that it couldn't be your fault, and now that I know that it wasn't, I am perfectly happy about it. As a matter of fact, it was really rather fun, especially to look back on, except, of course, the fumes, which were horrid."

"The fumes?" said Forbes, in rather a bewildered way. "What fumes were they? I haven't heard anything about that."

"Why," she answered, "poor Mr. Kent was nearly poisoned with them. We brought him out unconscious."

His attention thus called to me, Forbes turned and said, "Hullo, Kent!" at the same time cordially grasping my hand.

"It is evident," he said, "that there is still much which I haven't heard. That is perhaps hardly surprising, as most of what I know was gathered from the last two minutes in court, and my subsequent conversation with the police. Won't you tell me all about it?"

Here Lady Cheney interposed with the suggestion that as she and her daughter were equally anxious to hear about Mr. Forbes, and had no doubt that Mr. Kent was too, we should both join them at lunch at Cheney Park, where we could talk more comfortably. We gladly accepted the invitation, and moved to follow the ladies out of the room.

"Pardon me, sir," said a well-modulated voice behind us, and turning we beheld the grave visage of Mr. Albert Dean.

"Hullo, Dean," Forbes exclaimed, "I am glad to see you, but what brings you here?"

"I was summoned for the inquest, sir," said Mr. Dean. "Am I to prepare a bed at the cottage for you to-night, sir?"

"Well, no—or let me see, yes. Yes, rather. Prepare two beds. You'll come and spend the night with me there, Kent, won't you? You will? Good—we shall be more comfortable there than at the 'White Hart,' and there's nothing to do here now. But, Dean?"

"Sir?"

"How is it you haven't prepared as it is? I never told you I should be away for any time."

"No, sir, but as you instructed me to forward your letters to France, sir, I assumed that you would not be home immediately."

"To France, Dean?"

"Yes, sir. To Poste Restong, Le Havre. You telegraphed me from Southampton on Monday evening, if you recollect, sir?"

"Telegraphed, did I? Always distrust telegrams, Dean. There's no knowing who sends them."

"Certainly, sir. Here are the keys you sent me from Le Havre, or would you prefer me to keep them till you get home, sir?"

"Keys? Oh! yes, I see. Yes, I see. An ingenious scheme. Keep them for the present, Dean. We shall be over early this evening."

"You have your car with you, I assume, sir?"

"Lord, Kent," exclaimed Forbes, "I forgot all about that in the other excitements. I wonder where my car is? Somehow, I thought it would be at home. It isn't there, Dean?"

"No, sir. It has not returned since you left, when you went off with that young man, sir."

Quite clearly Mr. Albert Dean had from the first strongly disapproved of "that young man"; in which, apparently, he showed a sounder instinct than any of the rest of us.

"And it isn't at Cheney Park, I suppose?" Forbes reflected. "In a certain event, the fellow was to have reported there."

"I think it can't be," I said, "or I should have heard of it. I don't think you'll find it there."

"Southampton!" Forbes exclaimed suddenly. "That's where it will be, of course. Somewhere in Southampton. The police will find it for me with any luck. At a guess, I should say it will be found in a public parking-place, probably the big one near the theatre. In the meantime, Dean, be a good fellow, trot over to Worcester, and send me out a car from there as soon as possible, will you? Let him come to Cheney Park."

"Very good, sir," replied the imperturbable Dean. How he intended to get to Worcester was a mystery into which we forbore to inquire—a confidence which in this case, at any rate, proved later to have been justified.

We hurried after Lady Cheney and Mary, who were waiting for us outside with their car—the same little car which was associated with the beginning of our strange adventures. The dickey at the back was now open, and Forbes and I clambered into it. Mary took her place at the wheel, and Lady Cheney by her side, and we started off. The car made no trouble about covering the distance this time, but sped easily up the drive, and past the spot where by its former stoppage it had revealed the secret of a dastardly crime. Once more I reflected upon how small a thing may turn the whole course of many lives—a commonplace thought enough, in the abstract, but impressive in the concrete. Already my own life had turned to new horizons; strange adventures had befallen Mary, Cheney, and Forbes—what had happened to Forbes? I still wondered, not to speak of the criminal Shortditch, and that unspeakable reprobate, Cavendish—and all because of a tiny fragment of metal lodging by accident in a tube.

It was a windy March day, with a northwesterly breeze, which drove piled cumulus clouds sailing in stately procession across a bright sky, dappling the park and roadway with swiftly alternating sun and shadow. Forbes was sufficiently occupied holding on the notorious soft black hat, and I in nursing a pipe, from which glowing sparks streamed at intervals, and in reflecting on "fixed fate, free will, foreknowledge absolute"; though I fear my ruminations, if profound, were not very coherent, for I was distracted by the continuous flapping of Forbes's cape. Nevertheless, the ride in the air was refreshing after the close atmosphere of the village hall, and besides, this was the first time for several days when my mind was free enough from the excitement and anxieties of the case upon which

we had been engaged, to regain its normal poise. I felt
a pleasant sense of rest and freedom, and looked at the
spring landscape, as we sped past it, with delight. As to
the case, I supposed that we had nearly done with it.

The sunshine, as it happened, was streaming into the
dining-room at Cheney Park when we entered it, and
shone on a silver bowl of early narcissus on the centre
of the gate-legged table, and reflected it in the polished
surface. The dining-room was of the same general shape
as the library on the other side of the hall, and the large
windows faced in the same direction, looking out over
that clump of rhododendrons—a few already in flower—in
which Mary and I had thought we heard a movement when
she was going to tell me of the poor Professor's secret. I
was placed facing the window, with Forbes opposite me,
Mary on my left, and Lady Cheney on my right. Naturally
enough, we were all burning with curiosity to hear of
Forbes's adventures, for we all felt sure that something
out of the common must have happened to him since that
eventful morning—could it really be only two days before?
Lady Cheney asked him to tell us about it, as soon as the
maid had put the lunch on the table and left the room.

"I am afraid, Lady Cheney," he replied, "that you will
find my story long, and insufferably tedious, and once
I start telling it I see no hope of being able to devour
my fair share of these excellent veal cutlets. I am equally
curious to hear of Miss Cheney's experiences, which will, I
feel sure, prove far more entertaining than my own. To be
candid, I really didn't know how hungry I was until these
admirable cutlets recalled the fact."

"Poor Mr. Forbes," laughed Mary. "It seems as if starvation had been included in your adventures."

"A man cannot really starve," said Forbes, helping himself liberally to potatoes, "in less than a week at least. It is

quite possible to fast for a month, with excellent results. But fifty hours is certainly enough, I find, to produce a marked sensation of hunger."

"Fifty hours! Good gracious, yes," said Lady Cheney. "I should think it was. I had no idea of it! Now, Mr. Forbes, I insist upon it. You mustn't say another word. Will you take a little Burgundy? A whisky and soda?"

"Burgundy," said Forbes, "is the one thing needful. Thank you, Lady Cheney. Now, Miss Cheney, to complete your kindness, won't you tell me how much you have had to put up with, so that I may know the worst?"

"Really, you needn't concern yourself about me, Mr. Forbes," she answered, laughing. "I got off better than any one. I was taken a little ill in the car, and went in to Uncle Frank's house—I didn't know it was his then—and lay down on a bed. I must have gone to sleep. When I woke up I was still on the bed, but in the cellars, only I didn't know that, and so I didn't mind. Then when I did know, Mr. Kent was there, too, and looked after me. So really there was nothing dreadful. I am afraid poor mother had a worse time than I did, didn't you, mother?"

"Oh, well, my dear, I was anxious about you, of course, but I am afraid Mr. Kent had the worst of it. I hope you feel quite recovered now?" she inquired, turning to me.

I assured her that I never felt better in my life, and to turn the conversation, which I felt to be embarrassing, I remarked that I still couldn't puzzle out for the life of me, how the chauffeur had got hold of my address in London. Forbes looked at me and passed his plate for more cutlets.

"Come, Kent," he said, "you have no excuse for secretiveness. You had bacon and eggs for breakfast. Tell me what occurred."

I explained how his car had called for me on Monday evening, and taken me down to rescue Mary, and, in fact, the whole story up to our own rescue by Mr. Francis. "Now," I said in conclusion, "how can the man have discovered that address?"

"At first, I suppose," said Forbes, "you thought I had given it him?"

I agreed.

"But now," he continued, "that you know I did not—I gave it to nobody—it seems strange to me that you do not see the only possible solution, for the facts are surely simple. You revealed this address to me, no third party being present, and to nobody else; I destroyed it at once and I revealed it to nobody; yet a third party knows it."

"Exactly," I said, "that's just what makes it so difficult. Nobody overheard me give it you, and it wasn't mentioned again."

"If we were not overheard," he replied, "it follows we were overlooked. You wrote that address. You wrote it, as I recall now the question arises, with a sharp pencil over new blotting-paper. I have no doubt you left a perfectly legible copy there. My mind, at the time, was occupied with other matters, or I ought to have thought of it then. However, as it turned out, it was as well. I think, on the whole, it has rather played into our hands."

At this point the maid came in with the next course, and the subject was dropped, but I saw at once that Forbes's solution was perfectly feasible and doubtless correct—even obvious, so much so that I began to wonder why I had not thought of it myself. Shortditch doubtless noticed the address on the blotting-paper, knew that I had been there, and probably Forbes with me, and passed the news on to whoever else was interested. It was a bad blunder on my part, but, happily, the disaster to which it might have led was, it seemed, averted.

"It seems curious to me," said Forbes, sprinkling sugar over a baked apple, "that we all sit so much more calmly over a dormant volcano than we should on an anthill. I mean, that we are all very alive to the petty annoyances of modern life, but seldom trouble ourselves much about its dangers."

"I quite agree with you," said Mary. "It's the wretched little worries that really bother you. But what dangers do you mean? I hoped that was all over and done with."

"Don't be alarmed," said Forbes. "I really began by thinking about the annoyance of losing my car, and then of how dependent one is on these things. We depend on artificial means for our necessities. Machinery of all kinds is essential to the existence of millions of people, who are at the mercy, therefore, of the few who manipulate it, and that is getting to be so more and more. Or take the water supply. London, of course, is supplied from several sources. It might not be so easy to deprive London of water. But in the case of Birmingham, I can imagine an enterprising enemy finding no great difficulty. Our food position, similarly, is very insecure. Like Antaeus, we should be stronger if we came down to earth, but we can't even do that nowadays, without a lift."

"But you don't think England will ever be in danger of revolution do you, Mr. Forbes?" said Lady Cheney.

"If I wanted to set up a Bolshevist government in England," he answered, "I think I should try to avoid the ordinary method of red revolution. The only object of taking the masses into your confidence, in the first place, would be in order to seize power. Having seized it, you subdue the masses. It seems to me that a simpler course would be to seize power by means of peaceful penetration—assisted, preferably, by the possession of some very powerful weapon—and then you could drive the masses like a flock of sheep."

"Theoretically," I said, "that might possibly be so, but it is rather difficult to see how the peaceful penetration could be accomplished—at least to the extent necessary to get effective power. It's not practical politics."

"No," said Forbes. "It's the scheme of a madman; but should he happen to possess a weapon by which one man could destroy a city, I shouldn't be certain that the madman might not get his way. However, we may take it that before that happens he will be safely put away in an asylum."

In such generalities we avoided the explanation of his own doings which Forbes seemed reluctant to give. But I noticed that Mary remained thoughtful during the meal.

Soon afterwards the car arrived from Worcester and Forbes and I set out. I was longing to ask about his strange behaviour, but Forbes's manner was not encouraging.

21

NARRATIVE OF HORTON FORBES

Forbes had chosen for himself a charming retreat. It was a thatched cottage, set on a hillside above a little stream. Behind it was an orchard, and in front such a garden as, in summer, would be full of hollyhocks, snapdragons, Canterbury bells, and the hum of bees.

The interior was equally comforting. The room into which I was taken was of good size, though rather low, with old oak beams across the ceiling. Much of the wall space was occupied with books, gleaming cheerfully in the firelight. There were a few good etchings, and in a corner by the window a little water colour of Naples which took my fancy greatly.

Tea was immediately provided by Dean, and it was while we sat in deep easy-chairs before a cheerful blaze, that Forbes related to me the story of his startling adventures, which I have thought better to give in his own words, leaving out the exclamations and questions with which I interrupted him.

I will begin (said Forbes) at the time when I returned here and you went up to London to report to Channing our discovery of the chess cipher, and to make inquiries about V. S. Stephens.

Early on Sunday one of my homers, which I had sub-
stituted at the mill for one marked with the black mitre,
arrived at my cottage. It brought two things—the formula, as I believed—for it appeared to be in Sir William's
handwriting on a half-sheet of note-paper—and a typed
message on thin paper, in the chess cipher. This read,
when decoded in the way I hinted to you: "Yours received.
Expect you 31825 accordingly Q. Sq."

I was confident that Q. Sq. represents The Laurels.
Q. Sq. was the rendezvous indicated in the message in Sir
William's pocket. Still more convincing was the evidence
of the maps which I saw in the car at the mill. On one of
them small circles had been lightly marked at the intersection of lines eight squares apart. A chessboard was suggested, and I found that Q. Sq. (reading the board upside
down, as before) included Wilmer Deeping.

I also inferred that my cottage is near the centre of K.
Sq. With regard to the message itself, I thought it desir-
able that the meeting should be observed, and the conversation overheard, and made the necessary arrangements to
secure this. With regard to the formula, it was important
to get the handwriting identified immediately. I therefore
telegraphed to Miss Cheney, asking her to come over on
Monday in my car, which I would send for her at noon.
I considered it unwise to carry the formula about the
country, or even to remove it from my safe, without real
necessity.

At 10.15, however, on Monday morning, Thomas, Lady
Cheney's chauffeur, arrived at my cottage. He brought
a letter, ostensibly posted from myself to Miss Cheney.
It was typed, on thin paper, and my signature was well
imitated. It had been despatched at 6.45 p.m. on Sunday
at Stoke Beauchamp, my nearest office. It was post-marked
at Luttercombe at 7.50 a.m. on Monday. The envelope had
been opened.

The letter stated that, owing to a sudden development in the case, I had been obliged to alter my plans, that I should send a car at 9 instead of noon, and that I urgently requested Miss Cheney to meet me at Mr. Francis's house in the Black Mountains.

I had no doubt of the identity of Thomas, the new chauffeur, as I had seen him working in the garden at Cheney on my first visit there. Miss Cheney, he said, read the letter at breakfast, which she took alone, and left it open on the table. At 9 a.m. a car very like mine arrived. She got into it, and was driven away. As it passed down the drive, he noticed that the chauffeur was a young man whom he had often seen driving a limousine in the neighbourhood. He wondered, therefore, whether the car could have been sent by me. He mentioned this suspicion to Lady Cheney, whereupon she instructed him to come to me and verify the matter. So he cycled to the station, and just caught the train which arrives at 10.7.

This story was consistent with the facts, so far as I knew. But the situation was puzzling. Was the forged letter really intended to entrap Miss Cheney? No adequate motive for her abduction was known to me, although it might be possible that our antagonists would hope to use her as a hostage. If it were so, I must presume an unusual degree of intelligence, alertness, and loyalty in the new chauffeur.

Alternatively the letter was intended to entrap me, and might have no truth in it at all. The Black Chessmen could not, I thought, be aware of the full extent of the evidence against them which I have secured; but there was no doubt that my removal would be worth attempting, and I had reason to regard Mr. Francis's house with grave suspicion.

But owing to the fact, disastrous at this juncture, that there is no telephone at Cheney Park, I could not communicate with Lady Cheney. Immediate action was imperative, and it was impossible to let the consequences of

a wrong decision on my part fall on Miss Cheney. I felt
that the only course open to me was to follow her without
delay. If I could discover no trace of her supposed abduction, I hoped to be able to take sufficient precautions to
ensure my own safety. I might also obtain the opportunity
which I required for investigation of the house.

I sent all papers of value, including the formula, to the
Bank, by my man, Albert Dean. Thomas I took with me,
and kept him under observation. I drove, and he sat beside
me. There was nothing suspicious about his behaviour at
any time. In fact, I began to fear that his story was genuine, for I had nothing against him, except that he was a
newcomer, and that he could not dig.

I stopped at the cross-roads. I arranged with Thomas to
wait there for an hour, and if I did not reappear, to send a
wire to Channing. He was then to return to Cheney Park
and report. I suppose that he did none of these things. I
felt that some danger, which I could not define, was over-
hanging my helpers, but I dared not turn back.

I walked to the lodge at the entrance to the drive. I
was told, rather to my surprise, that Mr. Francis was away;
that nobody was in the house, which was closed, and that
no car had been seen that morning. There was a possibility
that Miss Cheney, having been enticed into the car, had
been taken to some other destination. There remained also
the possibility that the whole story was false.

I knew that it was feasible to get into the grounds from
among the derelict sheds at the side. I found the house
shut up. Shutters were over the ground floor windows,
and the rest were closed. The front and back doors were
locked. But on passing round the house, I found a side
door, which opened when I tried it. It led into a narrow
stone passage. On the left was a locked door, opposite was
another, which stood ajar. I pulled it open, and saw an

empty cupboard. It was of no interest in itself, but on the floor I saw a blue pendant.

In the dim light I could not see it clearly. But it recalled to my mind a very charming ornament belonging to Miss Cheney.

I stepped into the cupboard to pick it up. The door slammed behind me, and immediately the cupboard descended into the bowels of the earth.

When the cage or lift came to a stop, it was in a brick-lined shaft. Fortunately, I had my case with me, containing a number of useful things, amongst them an electric torch. I also had an automatic pistol in my pocket. The bricks were streaming with damp and covered with mildew; in places they had fallen away, in others they bulged ominously. There was no door to the cage itself, and there was a distance of a couple of feet from the front edge of the floor on which I stood to the wall opposite it. This gap was filled by a platform of what seemed to be sound and fairly new planking. It formed a bridge between two passages, some two and a half feet wide and not quite five feet high, which opened in the shaft wall on each side. I was not going to risk stepping out of the cage, however, without some precautions, having already had one rather drastic lesson, and I thought I would try first to discover the nature of the mechanism which worked it. If it should be a counterpoise, and I stepped out, the result would be that when the cage was freed of my weight, it would go up and leave me stranded.

There was no ordinary switch to be seen, but there were four large round-headed nails, apparently holding down a square of linoleum on the floor. In reality, however, they did no such thing. I found that it was possible to press each of them down, so that the top of the head was flush with the surface of the linoleum. They merely covered a hole in it, through which they could pass. Yet this discovery led nowhere—nothing happened, although by further investigation I found that the nails were connected with wires, and were undoubtedly electric controls. I fiddled with them for quite a long time, but eventually had to conclude that the current had either failed, or been cut off, and that I should have to make up my mind either to sit there till it was restored, or find some other way of dealing with the situation. I was not sure whether I had stepped on one of the bosses when I first entered the cupboard, and so set the mechanism in action. I thought not, but in that case it was difficult to understand what had caused the descent.

I replaced the switches as I had found them, to make sure that if the current were restored the cage would stay where I left it, and decided to explore. I first examined the platform with my torch. It looked quite sound. I then tested it with one foot, gradually putting more weight upon it, and finally, keeping a good grip of the sides of the cage, stood on it with both feet. It supported me quite firmly, so I returned and collected from my case a few things which I thought I might need. The case itself I left, because I was afraid it might hamper me. Since, for all I knew, I might be confronted with a sort of Cretan labyrinth, I began by tying a strong thread from a reel on a drawing-pin which I pressed firmly into the floor of the cage, and was then ready. But I was still suspicious of that platform. It looked so new, and I tried it again, further from the centre, holding on to the side of the cage with my left hand. With a sharp crack, it turned on its centre, like a seesaw, and before I could do anything it went bumping and plunging down the shaft. After several seconds there came an answering "plonk" and a muffled splash, from some two or three hundred feet below. As for me, I sat down suddenly on the edge of the cage, and only saved myself from following the planks by thrusting my right hand against the clammy wall opposite, and clinging hard to the cage with my left. The thing had been supported on a rusty iron bar which projected in the centre, and no doubt helped to support the original stage; but at each end it was held merely by wooden pegs driven into the remains of the rotten planks which were still left there. So there I was with my feet dangling over the edge, and the light of my torch was not strong enough to show me how far I should have to fall before I ended in the water.

Still it was no good staying where I was; to get into either of the two passages was now not easy, but more hopeful than sitting still. I selected that on the right hand, and gathering up my thread and clinging to whatever I could find, managed to step over the chasm and land safely. The air in the passage was even more unpleasant than in the shaft, damp, earthy, and rather foul, and the passage itself was low, narrow, and very roughly cut, through red sandstone, for the most part, and led downwards. I followed it for five minutes or so, and then suddenly came to a dead end. There were no side passages, and there was nothing for it but to go back and start again. If the other side were the same, the outlook would be gloomy. Rewinding my thread on its reel, I retraced my steps. When I reached the shaft, the cage had gone!

I was confronted with a gap of five or six feet, over a drop of two or three hundred. Such a gap is not very formidable; you can almost step across it, certainly jump it; but in this case the passage in which I stood was so low that I had to crouch, and the passage opposite was worse still, for though its top was at the level of the top of mine, its floor was higher than my floor. Jumping from a crouching position on to a higher level, where you must still crouch, presents difficulties. Besides, the bricks at the end of both passages were loose, and the earth which they still held in

place was soft and crumbling. I had dislodged some when
I got into the passage from the cage, and to take off from
it for a leap, or to try and straddle the gap, was to ask for
disaster. There remained the rusty iron bar projecting half
way across. It was a flat bar, and had been bent downwards
by the fall of the platform. As it was, it gave no foothold.
One would infallibly have slipped off it, for it projected less
than two feet, and was pretty sharply bent. I wrestled with
that bar, I should think, for the best part of an hour, and
blistered my hands badly in the process. I could have bent it
downwards fairly easily, for I could have put my weight on
it; but to bend it upwards was a Herculean task. At last I got
it nearly straight, but not quite. It was still bent downwards.
But I could do no more, for it was working loose. I should
have to attempt it as it was, for it was neck or nothing.

I have seldom experienced a more unpleasant moment
than when I finally braced myself, and stepped on to it
across the slimy gulf. As I set my foot on it, I felt it give,
and sprang for the other side. I landed on my left knee,
just on the edge, and clawed desperately at the ground.
My hands found a projecting stone which just supported
me; but, at the same moment, all the brickwork gave way,
and my knee slipped over the edge. The stone also began
to give; but by that time I had got my body flat in the
passage, and only my legs were dangling over the pit. The
passage unfortunately sloped upwards; nevertheless, desperation gave me unusual agility, and I somehow managed
to drag myself out of danger. It was a close thing; the
brickwork on both sides had gone clattering down, and
the iron bar as well. But for the presence of that stone, I
should infallibly have followed them.

After resting a while to recover, I tied my thread again
to the stone which had served me so well, and proceeded
on my way, which led gradually upwards through a passage
very similar to that on the other side. In this case, however,

there were numerous others branching off, and at one point there were four, radiating in different directions. My general principle was to continue upwards, and so I abandoned several which I tried when I found them beginning to descend. Without my thread, I should certainly have lost myself, for I had to turn back several times. At last I struck one of the four which seemed to be a continuation of the one which led from the shaft, and I was glad to find it higher than the others, so that I could walk almost upright, which was a relief. I followed it for what seemed a considerable distance—it may not have been more than a hundred yards—ascending gradually all the time. It ended in a small open space, from which two other passages led, and was faced directly opposite by a stone construction, in which was a narrow door. I seemed to recognise this as the lower part of that curious tower which we noticed behind the house; but it was, of course, a mere guess. Anyhow, I withdrew into my passage to consider. It had become plain that the cage did not descend and reascend so inopportunely for me by accident. I could not doubt that my movements there had been observed, and the mechanism worked by the observer. How he could have observed me, or whence, was what I had to discover; but all I could arrive at was that there must have been some device in the cage itself which indicated my entry and exit from it, so that it was impossible to tell whence it was controlled. Quite likely, I thought, from this very tower, from which, as I had now discovered, a secret way existed to the house. Should I enter it—supposing that I could? Well, the place called loudly for investigation, and I hardly thought that, considering the extreme difficulty I had found in reaching it, I should be expected there. A trap, I thought, would have been made a little more approachable—and trap or not, it was a chance which ought not to be missed, supposing that I could get in.

About that there was no difficulty. The door was covered with metal, once painted white, now stained and yellow. It had no keyhole, and was kept closed by a spring. It opened inwards, and holding it partially open, I examined the interior with my torch, which by this time was growing rather dim. What first caught my attention was a large circular pillar supporting the centre of the vaulted roof; then sweeping the light round, I saw a large cellar or vault, with a bricked floor, stone walls of great thickness, and, of course, no windows—the sort of place which a prudent man would think twice before entering. Accordingly I stayed where I was, keeping the door open with my left shoulder. What was surprising was that the vault seemed pretty dry, and was adequately, even comfortably, furnished, with table, chairs, and sofa, a sideboard, on which was an empty tantalus—and, stranger still, on a small table there was a chess-board with the pieces still in position, as if a game had been abandoned in the middle. I much wanted to examine that, but swinging my failing light still further round, I saw in a small curtained recess just to the left of the door a telephone! I could just reach one of the chairs from where I stood, so to make sure of avoiding accidents, I propped the door open with it, stepped into the recess, and took up the receiver. I suddenly felt very queer—I remember thinking vaguely it was reaction from the strain, and noting how far away my voice sounded as I gave the number. I heard a very tiny voice asking me to repeat it, and then everything went completely blank.

22
FORBES CONTINUES

When consciousness returned to me (Forbes continued), I found myself lying on the sofa. I came round quite quickly and easily, as if waking from sleep, and my head was clear in a few seconds. I at once saw that the chair had been replaced in its original position, and that the door was shut. On testing it, I found it fast, though no sign of any bolt or lock was visible. To open it was plainly impossible, and I had, as best I could, to stomach the knowledge that I had been trapped again. On feeling my pockets I found that my automatic had been removed, as well as all papers of any interest. My money, my reels of thread, my torch and my pocket camera and some other trifles were left me, but none of these seemed likely to be of much use, except the torch, for which I luckily had a refill. As the old battery was exhausted, I was proceeding to change it when I was startled by a singularly malign voice somewhere in the darkness above me. If the devil was to appear in the flesh, his words would, I am sure, have just such an intonation.

"Allow me to congratulate you, Mr. Horton Forbes," said this odious but invisible personage, "on your really very charming simplicity, and your highly entertaining feats of acrobatics. You will be a specimen worth examining."

As these words were spoken, I was suddenly dazzled by the illumination of an electric bulb which hung directly above my head. It was covered by an opaque shade, so that while it threw a powerful light on me, it cast a deep shadow over everything above it. It hung from the highest part of the roof, and in the obscurity I thought I could detect a patch of deeper shadow, from which, perhaps the sinister voice had come.

"You have afforded me much amusement," the voice continued. "You have given me the kind of pleasure which a cat feels on seeing the mouse come out of his hole, or which the spider must experience on observing the approach of a succulent fly. I always like my flies to come into the spider's parlour of their own accord, Mr. Forbes. I apply compulsion only to secure that they don't get out again."

There are few things more exasperating to a normal person than to be scrutinised by unseen eyes, and jeered at by invisible lips, but happily I am blest with an even temper. I lay back on the sofa and replied:

"Cats and spiders are, I am afraid, creatures which I find almost equally distasteful. They are both, however, accustomed to dally with their victims. May I ask how you have observed my movements, and how long you propose to amuse yourself with me?"

"I have constructed," he answered, "in my leisure hours, a system of electric signals, at once ingenious and simple. It enables me to know when any inquisitive person enters my lift, and when, and how, he leaves it. I am glad, on the whole, that my inadequately planned landing-stage did not deceive you. That would have been too abrupt a death, and would have deprived me of the advantage of your very pleasing conversation. It cannot be denied, however, that it would have saved me some trouble, and you a tedious delay. I have not yet decided how long I shall be able to entertain you here. At present, you do not greatly incommode me, and I am inclined to leave my basement at your disposal until I hear that your disappearance is properly accounted for to your friends outside. We shall then be able to arrange for you without interference."

"The compliment," I said, "is one which I appreciate. It is evident that you regard me as a danger to yourself."

"A danger," the voice replied coldly, "which has been removed. My feelings towards you, Mr. Forbes, are impersonal. You have interfered at a crisis in my plans, and have penetrated here, where even my own subordinates are excluded. I am aware that the people of this detestable country like to spy, from behind a mask of virtue, on their neighbours' sins; but the wisest of them spy in my interest, and not against it."

"You have then," I said, "some grudge against this country?"

"Twenty years ago," he said, "I was hounded out of it by a pack of hypocrites. I regret, Mr. Forbes, that I am obliged to sacrifice you in the attainment of my revenge."

The light was extinguished, and the voice ceased. Its owner had told me, perhaps, more than he intended, secure in the knowledge that I was in his power. The situation certainly seemed almost desperate, but I was not then ready to accept that. I closed the refill in my torch, and started investigation. I began with the chess-board. Had I not before found chess mixed up with this affair, I daresay I should have paid it no great attention, but it was a beautiful set. The board was formed by the bottom of a rather shallow sandalwood box, in which the squares were inlaid in ivory and ebony, and the pieces finely carved from the same materials. Each piece was fixed by means of a small projecting peg of its material into a hole in the square, and each peg had a band of gold round it—as I thought, at first. Really, it was copper. With such a set it would be possible to play in a gale at sea. The box itself formed part of the table on which it stood. To close it, you turned it a half circle to the left. The position of the pieces was curious, and seemed suggestive of clumsy play. I was examining one of the loose pieces, and admiring the exquisite workmanship of it, when I was again interrupted.

"While I am delighted," said the same voice, "that you should use all the liberty of a guest, even if uninvited, I have already pointed out that it is dangerous to meddle. You do so at your own risk."

I switched round my light to the spot from which the voice seemed to proceed, but the surface of the roof there was unbroken, and I could detect no aperture through which it could come. Why, anyhow, was this ubiquitous person concerned about his chessboard? What danger could I incur more threatening than I already faced?

But it would be better to explore free of his observation, so I decided to defer any further action till the night, when I hoped he would be asleep. Incidentally, I hoped also that I should be alive. In a place of this kind, one has little feeling of security. On looking at my watch, I was astonished to find it was not yet three in the afternoon, but I decided to sleep if I could. I lay down on the sofa and closed my eyes. Once the light was flashed on for a second, but I kept them closed. Soon afterwards I slept. When I woke it was nearly eleven—too early. I lay still some hours, thinking. Then I got up and began work.

Standing on the table, which brought my head quite near the roof, I searched for any aperture. There was none in the place where I expected it, and it was not until I looked in quite the opposite direction that I detected a slight difference in the tone of an oblong section just above the pendant light. Looking more closely, I saw that there was certainly an opening—rather larger than that of an ordinary letter-box—covered by metal whitened to correspond with its surroundings, and at present firmly closed. It was difficult to see what I should gain even if I could open it, for I should not even get a view, except of what was directly over it. It was large enough to put a hand and part of the arm through, but no more. However, I worked at it with my knife, and found that it was closed by a very simple device—nothing more than a spring boss—and I soon had the metal lid free.

Extinguishing my torch, I cautiously opened it. There was only darkness beyond. I felt its surroundings with my hand, and found that it was set at the bottom of an aperture about six inches deep, and that there was another similar lid at the top. I opened that with equal ease, and then encountered no further resistance. Listening, and hearing no sound, I switched on my torch, but I could see nothing, owing to the depth and narrowness of the aperture, but a certain amount of whitewashed ceiling. I left the slit open, for any ventilation is better than none and my cellar was already in need of it, and went on to look at the rest of the vault.

There were two switches by the door, but neither seemed to work. I was rather chary of the telephone, but cautiously tried it. As I expected, the line was dead—the instrument disconnected—but I no longer experienced any bad results. The fixture of it to the wall was made in an unusual way, for it was attached to a square board of dark polished wood, which was very firmly attached to the wall behind it by means of a large number of round-headed bolts. There were sixty-four of them, which seemed excessive. Yet they were quite firmly fixed and appeared to be genuine. The pillar supporting the roof was not of stone, but merely a metal cylinder.

That is all that my examination of the place yielded, and it was not very helpful. I couldn't help thinking that the chess-board had something more behind it. It might be a concealed switchboard, controlling perhaps some mechanism in the door, and yet it seemed an unlikely method of letting oneself out of a room. It would be more natural to find such a thing outside. But it would merely be a variation of an ordinary combination lock. If you adopt such a lock, you must of course be able to set the combination from either side of the door; and, further, there must be a device by which the combination is released, and returns to some ineffective arrangement as soon as it has been used. The difficulty about the chess-board was that, as far as I could see, it was bound to remain set. The men could not jump out of the sockets in which they were placed, and revert to those from which they had been taken.

Try as I might, I could get no further. No way remained of making my escape. I was fairly immured. But at least it would be better than nothing if I could see what was on the other side of the slit through which I had been watched—yet even that seemed hopeless. I could not cut away solid stone. By this time I felt hungry, thirsty and exhausted, and the foul air and dead, earthy smell of the vault oppressed me. Something was moving in the room above me.

(Forbes paused, and lit one of his long cigarettes. . . .) That was my blackest moment, Kent (he resumed). It was intolerable to feel oneself so helpless. Then I heard the whirr of the telephone, and the voice that I had heard before came to me distinctly through the opening. "Norton Cheney 75." (It was easy to guess whose number that would be.) "B.K. speaking. Who are you?" There was a fairly long interval then, during which he was apparently listening to an account, which seemed by his comments to be satisfactory; and it was during that interval that my mind opportunely recovered itself, and I saw what to do.

Look at this camera. You see it has a brilliant view finder, unusually large for the size of camera, and accurately

made. Yet I had had this admirable instrument in my
pocket all the time, and never had the sense to make use
of it. Fortunately my slow wit did not entirely betray me;
it worked, however, only just in time. I took the finder
off the camera, and attached it to a wire, taken from the
lampshade overhead. As I did so, the voice continued: "I
shall do my part. You need have no fear of his appear-
ing. Absolutely none. I am leaving here now till Thursday
morning. You will know by then, I suppose?"

Meanwhile I had taken off my shoes, and was climbing
on the table, just as the conversation finished. I cautiously
raised my amateurish periscope through the opening. It
was difficult to see at first, because the thing was upside
down; but when I got the hang of it I could see perfectly.
There was a tray of glasses, more than filling the view;
but by moving my instrument I gradually took in the surroundings. The opening was in a low zinc-covered shelf
running along one side of a very small room—hardly more
than a passage—at the end of which, to my right, was a
window, and the sun shining into it. Beneath it I made
out a solid writing-desk, and a figure sitting at it; but I
could distinguish very little against the light. Opposite
me on the wall was the telephone, with the same curious attachment; and beneath it a number of small electric
bulbs and switches. A little to the left was another chess-
board, exactly like the one below, and only a foot or two
away. I could see it distinctly in miniature, but luckily
did not stay to examine it, for just then the figure at the
table got up. There is nothing more conspicuous than a
photographic lens, especially when it faces the light, and
I hastily withdrew it. When I ventured to peep again, a
hand—that was all I could see—was arranging the pieces
on the chess-board; but I could see them clearly, and you
may be sure, took good note of their position. Having finished arranging them, the hand closed the box, which shut

up with a click. I waited no longer, intending to set up my chess-board too, before I should forget the scheme; but I had hardly reached the ground when I heard the click, as of a door closing, in the room above, followed by silence. He had gone.

I set up the pieces, in a state of some excitement. As I triumphantly inserted the last, I flashed my torch on the door. Not a sound, not a movement. It was as much locked as ever. But—the bosses on the telephone board had suddenly become movable, they could be depressed. That was really all, except that the door which opened was not where I expected. It was in the central pillar, and revealed an iron spiral staircase. I have bored you long enough—so I will only say that I soon found myself in the upper room, and having seen all I could there, I walked out of the front door.

23

COUNTER-ATTACK

So ended Horton Forbes's strange tale. The fire, as though until this moment it had been listening, now collapsed in red embers, and set sparks weaving fantastic patterns at the back of the grate. Forbes rose and restored it to a genial blaze.

"Thank the Lord," I exclaimed, "that you got out of it safely; and thank the Lord also that I wasn't in your shoes. I should have been completely bunkered in that vault. It seems to me that, if you were clever enough to get out of that, you could get out of anything."

"I am deficient," he replied, "in the matter of cocktails. Dean refuses to mix them. On the whole, I sympathise with him. But I can offer you, say, a mixed vermouth, or a sherry and bitters?"

I chose the latter. Dean was summoned, and without any manifest signs of condescension, produced what was required.

"Either I am stupid," I said, "which I am by nature— or else this case still remains very mysterious. The only things that seem to me pretty certainly established are that the loathsome Shortditch murdered the Professor, and that the equally loathsome Francis put him up to it. Also, of course, that Cavendish is mixed up in it somehow. But as to the general idea of the gang, or what they are all after,

I am very vague. We seem to know nothing definite about any of them; and I really don't see how we ever shall."

"But what a pessimist!" said Forbes, laughing. "Let me just sum up what we know already, and I think you will see that things are not as bad as you think. Let us begin with the Professor. We find him communicating with, and receiving cryptic messages from, a criminal gang, and using their secret cipher. He was known to them, in fact, as the Queen's Knight. He was, therefore, a member. But as he was also a highly honourable man, it is reasonable to suppose that the real nature of the Society was unknown to him. He was duped. By whom, and for what purpose? Clearly by Cavendish. We heard that Cavendish had recently made his acquaintance on a pretext, and that they used to discuss science and philosophy together. We know of no one else who was both a friend of Cheney and a member of the gang. In actual fact, before I knew anything of Shortditch, I had suspicions of Cavendish. It was in connection with him that I was out on the night of the Professor's death, and it was for him that the message which my pigeon brought me here was intended. His rank in the Society is that of King's Bishop. The purpose for which he introduced the Professor is equally clear. It was to obtain the formula for the Society. No doubt it was at first intended to cheat him into parting with it. He must have refused, and it then became necessary to put him out of the way. The person chosen for this part was Shortditch, whose title is that of Queen's Bishop—ranking next to Cavendish, from whom, probably, he takes his immediate orders.

"So that accounts for three pieces. We can neglect pawns, I think, as likely to be subordinates who could know little of what was really intended, and that leaves us five to find. I don't intend to hunt all these up personally. That map which we found in the car Shortditch used was so marked as to indicate a square comprising eight map squares to a side—it was in fact a chess-board, and will give the police the clue where to look. The one piece which it is important to secure is plainly the King—perhaps also the Queen.

"I know pretty well where the King was to be found last Monday, and I hope to know still more about him next time we meet—which should be tomorrow evening. The two Bishops we have already, and once we bag the King I don't think much will be left. As to the Queen, she has not so far exposed herself. She is a power in the background, and I don't at present know who she is. I am hoping to get at her through the King, but I must admit that my complete ignorance about her is far from satisfactory. I assume that she is a woman, though that is perhaps to be too fanciful with the symbolism; but there has been a remarkable absence of women in connection with the members we know. Cavendish is a widower; so, by the way, is Francis; Shortditch is a bachelor, and I know of no one else."

"Could it," I suggested, "by any possibility be Mrs. Brook-Sutton?"

Forbes sprang up, and went to a book-case.

"Why!" he exclaimed, "that's an idea. She would fill the bill. But what made you think so? I haven't come across her anywhere in connection with this case. But stay! was she not mentioned as owning The Laurels?"

"I think she was," I said. "Also I have discovered that it was on her recommendation that Lady Cheney engaged Thomas as her chauffeur."

"But, my dear man," said Forbes enthusiastically, "that is a most valuable piece of information. That's the second time you have made an important discovery. We may, at least, take it as a working hypothesis that in recommending Thomas she knew something of the part he was to play. Let's see what *Who's Who* has to tell us. Ah! yes, this will be

it. Edward Brook-Sutton, member of the Stock Exchange,
et cetera . . . here we are 'Married in 1908 Mabel, daughter of Frank Francis, The Cedars, Kingston-on-Thames!'
Is Mrs. Brook-Sutton Francis's daughter, or is it another
man of the same name, I wonder? Let's see Francis. H'm,
no good. He isn't there. Well, it certainly looks as if she
had some connection with the business after all. And undoubtedly, she's the sort of person who could bring grist
to the mill."

"Exactly what do you mean by that?" I inquired.

"Well, I have formed a general notion of the principle
on which this gang works, and it seems to me a natural
inference from what we know, but if you think I am wrong,
correct me. Let me remind you, first, of what the invisible
voice said to me the other day—that in a country where
every one likes to spy on other people's misdeeds, the
wisest spy in his interest. What does that suggest to you?"

"To me," I said, "it strongly suggests some kind of
blackmail."

"I am glad, for it suggests the same to me. It was also
said that he was out for revenge, because he has been
hounded out of the country. That implies that money is
not his first consideration. The weakness of most blackmailing schemes is that they exist to extort money, and
that is the rock on which they usually split. If we assume
a blackmailer, to whom money is not an object, who may
indeed be already wealthy, he could, I should think, if he
worked skilfully, achieve a good deal in the direction of
revenge. But I gathered that his hatred was directed, not
so much against individuals, as against the country as a
whole. A tall order of course, but it might put a different
complexion on the acquisition of the Professor's formula,
which is a weapon of extreme deadliness. Instead of selling
it, for instance, to a foreign government, as one naturally

would expect such a gang to do, or attempt to do, it is conceivable that he intends to use it himself."

"But in that case," I objected, "what profit would Shortditch and the rest of the crowd get out of it? Why should they do all the dirty work, except for some jolly good reward?"

"One could imagine either that they are afraid to refuse, or they are well paid, or more likely both. Why shouldn't they be blackmailed, as well as be blackmailers, themselves?"

"Yes, that's very possible. It seems a pretty beastly form of business."

"Filthy. But if we are right, it is only necessary to remove the head, and the body will disintegrate. I believe I know several people who will be relieved."

"And how do you propose to remove the head?"

"If my car comes to-night, as I hope, I thought of running over to Black Mountains before daybreak."

"What?" I cried. "You don't mean to tell me you are going back to that infernal tower? You mustn't do it! Dash it all, I should have thought you would have had enough of that. Anyhow, if you go, I go with you."

"No, Kent; you've done your bit. It's time you got back and had some fishing at Cheney Park. This is my business."

"I refuse," I said. "If you go, I go with you, and that's flat. How do you suppose I could calmly go off fishing while you stick your head into the lion's den? Besides, I am as interested in this job as you are. The blighter tried to gas me, anyway, and I shall be jolly pleased if I see you get even with him. When do we start?"

"About two, I think. Better not be seen getting into the car. If you are really determined to come, let me say that I shall be immensely glad to have you—quite apart from the fact that two pistols are better than one. I think we shall come as an unwelcome surprise to our blackmailing Black King in his black mountains."

"He sounds," I said, "when you give him his full style and title, exactly like an ogre in a fairy tale."

"Well you will be Jack the Giant Killer, in that case. And talking of ogres, Kent, it's a strange thing, but I am still extraordinarily hungry. If Dean doesn't soon serve dinner I shall turn ogre myself and bite his head off."

"Dinner is served, sir," said Dean.

24

THE DANE'S TOWER

At three o'clock of a March morning the Dane's Tower is a lonely and sinister place. As we stumbled over the broken ground among the derelict buildings of the old mine, it looked grey and ghostly against its background of gaunt and sinister hills. A fitful wind whispered in the dry bents about our feet, with occasional gusts that came moaning out of the distance and passed in a spatter of rain. Overhead moved silently a dim procession of misty clouds, and the turning mill-wheel seemed like the trampling of an army.

From outside, the Tower looked as grim and deserted as the rest of the landscape. We climbed a few uneven, moss-covered steps, and at the top we were confronted by a wooden door from which the paint had long since peeled. Crouched in the darkness by it was a lean half-starved cat, mewing pitifully. When Forbes opened the door, which he did without difficulty, it followed us inside. It was a black cat—and black cats are said to be lucky—but it was mangy and horrible, and its presence was welcome to neither of us.

We found ourselves in an oblong room, the door being in the middle of the longer wall. It was fitted with electric light, and luxuriously furnished, but we did not use the light for fear of betraying our presence, and confined ourselves to our electric torch. There were six narrow

windows, four in the wall through which we entered, and
one in each side wall, set in masonry nearly three feet
thick. At the extreme left of the wall opposite was a hanging curtain; and towards this we went (dragging the now
familiar Gladstone bag) and followed by the mewing cat.

Behind the curtain was a door, through which we
passed. It opened into a small lobby, used as a pantry
apparently. On the wall immediately on our left, beneath
another narrow window, was fixed a square board with
numbered pegs, such as is used sometimes in hotels for
keys. On one of the pegs, a bunch of keys was hanging; on
another a dirty old cap. The rest of the lobby was fitted
with shelves, from hooks on which were suspended cups,
jugs and so on. As no exit was to be seen, I wondered why
Forbes had come here. He was standing with his back to
me at the board—looking, I supposed, for a key—and I
was on the point of asking him, when he suddenly took
hold of one of the shelves, and gave a gentle pull. A concealed door opened out, through which we passed.

The place in which we now stood was singular, rather
suggestive of a signal cabin. It was a fairly long room,
looking lofty because of its narrowness, for it was only
about six feet wide. The walls were of whited stone. That
containing the door was otherwise blank. In the right-hand
wall, immediately on my right as I stood in the doorway,
was a formidable safe; beyond it a blank space, and then
a square projection, protruding two or three feet. Beyond
that again was a low zinc-covered shelf, with a sink in the
middle, on the near side of which were glasses, decanters,
and bottles; on the far side, various beakers, bottles with
rubber stoppers and glass retorts. At the far end, beneath
a window was a solid writing-desk. All the windows in this
room, I noticed, had been covered over with metal shutters made like Venetian blinds, so that plenty of air came
in, but little light could get out.

The left-hand wall was even more extraordinary. It was blank near the door; just opposite the projection another board with numbered pegs was secured to it, and beyond that was an electric switchboard, with switches neatly arranged and lettered, and a row of electric bulbs, also lettered, of different coloured glass. Beyond these, near the writing-desk, was a telephone. There were two green-shaded reading-lamps, and a pendant from the ceiling, concealed by a hanging bowl of some translucent material, like fluorite. Almost in the centre stood a small table of Oriental workmanship, on which was the closed sandal-wood box that contained the chess set, of which Forbes had spoken. He, meanwhile, had switched on one of the reading-lamps, and put it on the floor to illuminate the safe. He took out of the bag, and fitted together, a remarkable apparatus, consisting of cylinder and tubes, which I learnt was to produce an oxy-acetylene jet.

"Unfortunately," he said, "our friend did not rely on his combination lock for this. We have to depend here on the ordinary methods of burglary." So saying, he put on a pair of dark goggles and stout gloves, explaining that the apparatus was fitted with a cutting blow-pipe, having two flames—one, oxyacetylene, and one pure oxygen.

Suddenly a brilliant flame hissed out, and gradually began to cut through the thick metal, as if it had been paper. Before very long a good piece of solid door had been cut away, though not without raising unpleasantly the temperature of the confined space in which we stood. After an interval Forbes inserted his arm, and began to withdraw the contents, while I watched with growing interest.

"Hullo," he exclaimed suddenly, "what's this? A marriage certificate! John Orme Lewison and Mabel Francis, at Chessington, in July, 1903. That's rather strange! Here is Mrs. Brook-Sutton cropping up again, Kent! I had no idea she had been married previously. More remarkable still, the officiating minister was Fielding Shortditch! Ah! this is even more to the purpose. Queen's Knight—Formula and Tests, carried out by King's Knight. That will repay study. And this. Nordensen's Death Ray—that's the young Norwegian scientist I mentioned to you. So I was right after all. His disappearance was connected with these others—Tests and experiments by K. So he trusted no one else with that!"

Numerous other documents came out—cheque books on twenty or thirty different banks, bonds, bundles of notes—and, at last, a solidly bound book fastened with a clasp. Forbes looked at it, and uttered an exclamation.

"We were right," he said. "Here are the names of scores, or rather hundreds, of people—names I know, too, many of them—with a short synopsis of their lives, and—this is the point—their most intimate secrets. Rather unpleasant secrets, I see. Well, I shall not examine that now. Here is something else—another book. By Jove! Kent, I believe this is the best find of all. It's in cipher, but it seems to be a list of the gang, and all about them. You see, here are various chess symbols. I must look into this. I wish, though, that I could remember in what connection I have heard the name Lewison. It is vaguely familiar. I can call no details to mind. Can he, by any possibility, be the man we are looking for?"

"Hardly, I should think," I answered, after a little reflection. "Since his wife has married again, is it not more natural to suppose that he is dead?"

"That certainly is a probable inference. On the other hand there might have been a divorce. It is strange that I haven't yet come across anything which reveals our man's identity. All these bankbooks, you see, are in different names—whether genuine or fictitious—and all the securities seem to be in the form of bearer bonds. There are no share certificates, which would be made out in the owner's name. However, I expect we shall find something when we can look through the material more carefully. And we may find more in the writing-desk."

The desk, however, although providing much that was useful, and still more that was not, did not disclose anything bearing on the point in question. All this search, which I have described as briefly as possible, had naturally taken a considerable time. Our plan had been to secure such evidence as we could find, and leave before it was light. We intended, if we were successful, to return later, in company with the police, and ensure the capture of the criminal, who was expected back some time later in the day. I found it was already past five. I called Forbes's attention to this fact.

"Yes," he said, "we had better be off. I suppose it's just possible that our man may, like Shortditch, come back earlier than we expect; and if he comes in during our absence he may alter the combination, and in that case we should find it difficult to get in again; so we may as well forestall him in that."

"How," I asked, "do you propose to manage it?"

"The alteration of one piece on the chess-board would be enough. First, however, I will just put our trophies in the Gladstone, and then we shall be ready to leave."

He proceeded to do so, kneeling on the floor close to the safe, and with his back to it. I stood opposite, watching him. The lean cat continued to prowl about the room uneasily, as it had done all the time. Suddenly I saw what for a moment kept me dumb with surprise, and a sudden chill of fear came over me. Then, recovering my wits:

"Look! Forbes, quick," I whispered, "quick! The wall behind you!"

Stealthily, and quite silently, the wall was opening! Forbes sprang up as I spoke, and with one stride placed himself beside the gap, pistol in hand. For a second I remained stupidly standing where I was, but he soon re-called me to my senses.

"Go round by the door, Kent," he said, quietly, "and take up a position on the other side of this. Keep out of sight."

I did as he directed, and placed myself on the far side of the gap which had so unexpectedly revealed itself, and which, we could now see, was produced by the sliding of a metal panel. There I waited with a quickened pulse for what would happen next.

Unless there were more than one to come through the hidden door, we were in a very strong position, since we each had an automatic, and were prepared; and even if there were more, we were still well off, for the gap was only wide enough for one to pass at a time. Still, it was nervous work, and the seconds of waiting seemed like minutes. From somewhere there came a distant hum, which sound-ed as if it proceeded from some subterranean depths; and cold air, smelling damp and earthy, streamed into the now warm room; but there was no sound of footsteps. Then as stealthily as it had opened, the sliding panel closed again. No visible trace of it remained.

We lowered our pistols, and I looked at Forbes in be-wilderment.

"Whatever can be the meaning of that?" I exclaimed.

"I am afraid," he answered, "it means that he has re-turned, and that our presence here is discovered."

"But we can't have been seen," I objected. "I had a view of the length of the passage before I moved; and there was no one there."

"I fancy, all the same, that I am right," he replied, "and our best course will be to get outside. He is not likely to come in now, and may escape altogether. It will take me a minute or two to finish, and then we will go."

I confess that I was relieved by this decision. I greatly preferred to deal with our unseen enemy in the open. And

I suppose my nerves were getting frayed, for I began to find the continual mewing of the wretched cat intolerable.

"What on earth can I do," I said aloud, "to stop that infernal row?"

"Get it some milk," said Forbes laconically, stowing things methodically in the Gladstone bag.

I had seen a jug of milk in the lobby, just outside the door, which we had left ajar; so I slipped out, and returned with a saucerful, letting the door swing to behind me. I set it on the chess table, followed very closely by the cat, mewing louder than ever. It immediately sprang on to the table; and in the very act of landing on it, it suddenly froze into immobility, and remained with lowered head, and one forepaw uplifted. The sight was uncanny, and rather horrible, and drew from me a sharp exclamation. Forbes looked up and saw what had happened.

"Had it touched the milk?" he asked.

"No," I said, "it had not. It stiffened like that in the very act of landing on the table. It never touched the milk at all." And I moved forward to examine it.

"Stop!" said Forbes. "Better wait a minute, Kent, and let me think. The table doesn't seem to be a very healthy spot. I should keep away from it."

Presently he went on: "We are dealing here with some other devilish arrangement, but I don't quite know what it is. The animal would scarcely look like that if it had been electrocuted. But I am afraid it means that we must leave our friend's combination alone, and depart with the booty. I see you have closed the door. No matter—it is only a question of . . . Hallo!"

This exclamation was caused by the sudden failure of the electric reading lamps, which both went out simultaneously, leaving us in inky darkness. We had our torches, so that this was not very serious, though it was annoying and strange, and by the light of his torch, Forbes proceeded to manipulate the numbered pegs on the board fixed on the wall. There was a set look on his face when he turned round, and said to me:

"They are immovable, Kent. Some one has cut off the current."

"What does that mean?" I asked with apprehension. "Does it affect anything but the lights?"

"It means," he replied, "that we can open none of the doors."

"A cheerful look-out," I said, with more gaiety than I felt, "with windows like these, and walls three feet thick. Any chance of a rescue by the police?"

"Do you notice," he asked, disregarding my question, "a kind of very dim violet glow on that chess table? To me it is only occasionally perceptible—as the squeak of a bat is to some people—and I am not sure whether it's real or imaginary. No, don't go nearer. Come over here behind this projection. Do you see it?"

"Like you, I have a sensation, very faintly—but I should have put it down to the effect of the sudden darkness—a complimentary colour from something we have looked at."

"It seems almost too faint for that; and it seems to me to be spreading, or else my eyes are getting more sensitive. I can distinguish it by the wall, as well. Can it be some kind of ray, which is near the violet end of the spectrum?"

"Nordensen's Death Ray, for instance?" I hazarded.

The suggestion carried conviction, for there was something very sinister about this light that was no light.

"It cannot reach us in this corner," he continued. "As long as we stay here I think we shall be all right."

Although it grew no stronger, and illuminated nothing, there was no doubt that the glow was spreading. It seemed to pervade the air. No objects became visible: only the darkness around us, instead of being black, took a dim violet tinge, which extended slowly. It was as if whatever instrument projected it were being slowly moved forward down a tube—reaching at first only a small circle, and gradually increasing as it approached the end of the tube, when it would radiate in all directions.

Meanwhile Forbes switched on his own torch, and keeping carefully in the corner, began to take things out of the Gladstone bag. I wondered how he could bother with them at such a time, and in such a danger. I was trying to compose myself to face our fate with resignation, for I could see no possibility of escape: absorbed in painful thoughts, I paid little attention to him.

Suddenly I was startled by the brilliant flame of the oxy-acetylene jet. The ruse was so simple really, and yet I had never thought of it. He was cutting through the sliding panel.

The metal was not thick, and it was a matter of moments only before the whole panel was cut clearly away, revealing to our torches a very narrow passage at a level a foot or two above the floor, and about ten yards long. I entered first—we both had rubber shoes—and Forbes followed, occasionally switching on his torch. The Gladstone bag we had perforce to leave behind. At the end of the passage was a square opening in the floor, on the near side of which was fixed a vertical iron ladder, descending to some unknown depth. In the angle of the wall and roof was a mirror, so arranged that from beneath it a view of the room we had just left was plainly indicated—although at that time we could not see it, for the room was dark.

At this point Forbes took the lead, and we proceeded with caution to descend the iron ladder. The worst of it was our ignorance of where we were going, combined with the almost certain knowledge that some one was lying in wait in the obscurity below. We dared not show a light, and had to feel for our footing in black darkness. Nothing happened, however, and at last we reached firm ground.

The droning hum, which I mentioned before, had been growing more and more in volume. We felt our way into another passage, equally narrow, which led straight for a little way, and then turned at right angles. As we came to the turn a light became visible, and the end of the passage. The light shone from some open place, from which the humming noise also seemed to proceed, mingled, as we could now discern, with a noise like that of petrol engines. We stopped, and Forbes whispered in my ear:

"I think the iron ladder was in the interior of the outer wall on the right of the tower, and if so we must now be going in the direction of the main building. This is evidently the power station. I expect to find our man there. If there is any cover in the place we must aim at getting the other side of him, to prevent his getting away by any exit there may be at the other end. You stay at this end of the passage, and I will try to steal round without being seen. As soon as I am in position, we will go for him simultaneously."

Agreeing to put this plan into operation, and taking every precaution, we crept silently to the end of the passage. Before us was a room with a concrete floor and brick walls, lit with unshaded lights. Down the centre ran a double row of dynamos, driven by petrol engines. At an elaborate piece of mechanism near the middle of the left wall stood a weird figure enveloped completely in a costume resembling that of a diver, with tinted goggles over the eyes. He was entirely unaware of us, and was absorbed in manipulating the apparatus.

Forbes, crouching low behind the humming dynamos, had got halfway across when the figure turned suddenly. I saw that he had caught sight of Forbes. I called sharply: "Hands up." Forbes sprang up at the same time, covering him with his automatic. Up went the man's hands—or rather one of them. The other went like lightning to a switch, and plunged us in darkness.

We both had our pistols in our right hands, and it was a second or two before we could get our torches in action. But in the meantime, the man had vanished, and by the time we were sure of it, he had got a fair start. After him we dashed, Forbes leading, down another passage at the far end of the room which echoed with a strange clanking and rumbling.

Suddenly from the darkness in front of us broke a sharp cry, followed by a succession of the most unearthly and horrible shrieks to which it has ever been my fate to listen; equally suddenly they were cut off in mid-utterance, and but for the monstrous clanking there was silence.

Rather shaken, we went on, through the damp and slimy tunnel, and came out in an underground chamber, nearly the whole of which was filled by cumbrous machinery, rusty but working, its groanings and clankings mixed with a dull roar of water. A heavy piston rose and fell in a sort of pit beneath it; above it passed some rotten wooden steps, which had broken; and broken not long before.

As we threw the light of our torches on the rusty rods and wheels, we saw, caught in one of them, a large fragment of the strange dress which our late enemy had been wearing; and as the heavy piston rose to its highest, we saw on it a great splash of blood.

Sick with horror, I turned away. Better to have been shot, than torn and ground to pieces in this horrible place; as our enemy must have been. Hypocrite and murderer though he was, I would not have condemned him to that fate. But such was the death allotted to him. For us, at any rate, the danger was over. The chase was at an end.

25

CHECKMATE

For some time Forbes remained silent. Finally he said:

"I want to make sure that I have overlooked nothing relevant in this extraordinary episode. But Channing and his officers will probably be here soon, if they have not arrived already, and one of us at least ought to meet them. Would you mind, Kent? Thanks, then. That will give me time to clear things up here. Go back, will you, by the way we came?"

I had no knowledge where to look for Channing, and Forbes did not give me time to ask; but I had little doubt that the Inspector would make for Mr. Francis's house. Accordingly, I climbed back up the iron staircase, and found the door from our late prison open. Evidently Forbes had restored the current. It was still dark when I emerged, though there were signs of dawn.

As I approached the front door of the house, I was startled by a light which was flashed on me from within.

"Oh! it's you, Mr. Kent!" It was Channing's voice. "What have you done with Forbes?"

I explained briefly. Forbes had remained behind, but would shortly follow me.

"Good," said Channing, apparently much relieved. "Then I need take no drastic action. We got no response to our ringing and knocking, and in the end we had to make our own entrance. What can have become of Mr. Francis, do you suppose?"

"There is no room for doubt about that," I replied. "He is dead."

And I drew a vivid picture of the final scene in the subterranean power house and told of the horrible shrieks we heard from amid the clanking machinery. Just then, from somewhere near sounded a soft footstep, and there was a low creak from the heavy door at the back of the hall.

Instantly three police lamps were flashed upon it; and standing framed in the doorway, to my utter bewilderment and horror, I saw none other than Mr. Francis himself. For a moment, I must confess, although I am not superstitious, I was ready to believe that it was his ghost! But Channing's voice cut into the silence that fell on all of us.

"Mr. Francis, I believe?"

The figure in the doorway nodded, without speaking. He was holding a lamp in his right hand.

Channing resumed: "I am Inspector Channing, of the Criminal Investigation Department, Scotland Yard. Will you explain, sir, why no response was given to our ringing and knocking?"

"It was not heard," was the answer, scarcely audible.

"How was that? Have you been out?"

Since the torches' showed, behind the standing figure, a spiral staircase descending, concealment was impossible. But he tried a subterfuge.

"I went down to the cellars," he said.

"And why?" snapped Channing.

Mr. Francis hesitated. The strain had told on him. He looked old and weary.

"I cannot tell you," he said at last.

"You refuse to give me any information?"

"Yes," said Mr. Francis firmly.

"Then," said Mr. Channing, "there is only one course open to me. I must detain you on suspicion of . . ."

"Unnecessary, Channing," said Forbes's quiet voice. "I will be responsible for Mr. Francis." He walked across and laid a hand on the old man's shoulder.

"Come, sir," he said gently, "I am happy to be able to tell you that your persecutor is dead. You have no more to fear from Caspian Orme."

Mr. Francis let the lamp fall. It rolled over and went out.

"Dead!" he whispered. "Dead! How do you know this, sir? How do you know what this means to me?"

"I will explain," Forbes answered, "But you must spare yourself, sir. Will you take us somewhere where we can sit and talk quietly?"

He showed us to his study. Forbes stretched himself out in an easy-chair, lit a cigarette, and asked the old gentleman to tell us his story.

"My relief at what you have told me," began Mr. Francis, in rather tremulous tones, "is so intense that I hardly know if I shall be able to give you a clear and orderly narrative.

"My troubles began many years ago, with the death of my dear wife. I was then quite a young man, in a subordinate position at the War Office. I was left with my daughter Mabel—my only child. You will be able to understand that she had a double share of my affection. I was always quiet and unambitious. Neither quality was congenial to her. She has been, from quite a child, fond of pleasure and society, determined to be noticed. I have felt that I am much to blame.

"Well, when she was a girl of twenty-two, she became involved in what seemed to me an undesirable friendship with a young man named John Orme Lewison. He was of

partly foreign parentage, but possessed the highest intellectual gifts. In fact, he was regarded as one of the most
brilliant young barristers of that day. Mabel, I think,
imagined that the success of his career would equal his
ambition; and no doubt it might have done so, had his
personal character been other than it was. But it came to
my knowledge early, and was later generally known, that
conduct of a disgraceful character was attributed to him.
He ceased to be received in Society, and was obliged to
resign from his clubs. Eventually he was disbarred. From
that moment he disappeared.

"That my daughter's relationship with him amounted
to anything more than friendship was at that time unknown to me. Although I was greatly relieved when she
promptly threw him over, her callousness about it was a
shock to me. It was believed that he went to the East, but
no one ever heard from him.

"After that Mabel launched out into a life of gaiety
which it was quite beyond my means to provide for. She
became the leader of a certain set of people, and was constantly entertaining and visiting these friends and we began, much to my sorrow, to become strangers to each other.

"So, when she told me by letter that she intended
to marry a Mr. Brook-Sutton, who was, I understood, a
wealthy stockbroker, it would have been useless to demur.
The marriage duly took place. Neither before nor after it
did Mr. Brook-Sutton show any wish for the acquaintance
of his father-in-law, and Mabel and I drifted still further
apart. But my affection for her remained, and remains.

"It was not till last year that I was dealt the crushing
blow. At that time—you may remember it—there came to
England a man of uncommon personality, reputed to have
made a fabulous fortune in China. He called himself an
American, and passed by the name of Caspian Orme.

"You will have guessed, gentlemen, that this was the John Orme Lewison who had left England in disgrace.

"But what you may not have guessed, and what I only learnt then at last from my own daughter, was that she had married him—secretly married him—just before his disaster. Imagine what a terrible blow this was to me! But even that was not all. I had a letter from Mabel, in which she said that she had met Orme at some house party. He had recognised her, and had asked her help. She had agreed to give it, without extreme reluctance, as it seemed, though he had threatened her with exposure if she refused. She told me this, and begged me to acquiesce in what her husband asked of me also. And indeed, it seemed little enough. It was merely that I should retire to this house, and see to the despatch and reception of certain pigeons, which, I was told, were used for communication on financial matters. Mabel was at the scoundrel's mercy, and, though with misgiving, I agreed.

"A little later I was given, through Mabel, an invitation to join a small circle of scientific and business men, whose object was, for the welfare of humanity, to suppress or control dangerous inventions. It is a matter in which I am deeply interested, and in spite of not knowing the names of the other members, I consented. I realised that secrecy would be necessary, and approved of it in such a case. In this instance it was secured by the use of chess symbols. I was to be referred to as the Black King's Knight, and I was told that if a meeting were necessary, it would be located in some chess square, according to a plan of which I should have previous notice. But in fact, I have heard no more of it from that day to this.

"Nor have I seen Lewison—Orme as he called himself—since many years ago, or had any direct communication from him until to-night. I was awakened by the telephone.

It was Orme speaking. He said that he was in imminent danger of his life. If I would come immediately to Dane's Tower, I could be of great service to him. In return he would hand over to me all evidence of his marriage to Mabel, and would leave us free.

"I went, taking a lantern with me. When I got to the tower, I found the door open and the light burning, but no one in the room. There was a staircase leading down to a cellar, and I went down. Still there was no one there. But at that point my memory becomes vague. I sat down. I suppose I must have slept. I awoke to find the place in darkness, and in my pocket I found, not the marriage certificate, but a chemical formula, and a plan of underground passages, the existence of which I had never imagined, leading from Dane's Tower to this house. The door by which I had entered the cellar had been closed. It resisted all my efforts to open it, and I had no alternative but to follow the plan which I found in my pocket. That is all the explanation I can give. I am utterly at a loss to understand what Lewison wanted, or why he spoke as he did. But what I have told you, however unintelligible, is the truth."

"I think it becomes quite intelligible," said Forbes, throwing away his cigarette, "in the light of what I know already. This last devilry of Orme's is of a piece with all the rest of this sinister conspiracy. He has been, since my escape, and his failure to get, with the assistance of Cavendish, a verdict against me at the inquest, in grave danger, and he must have known it. But he had guarded himself astutely. He had concealed his own existence with surprising cunning; he had arranged every circumstance to throw suspicion on you. You were to live here, in the centre of the web; you were to be responsible for the pigeon post; you were, in fact, admitted to the secret society of the Seven Black Chessmen. About that Society you were deceived, like Professor Cheney, but your membership was a fact which would have told very heavily against you.

"To-night, as I believe, expecting another visit from me, and perhaps from the police, Orme returned earlier than he had intended. His object was, in the first place, to make the chain of evidence against you unbreakable, and then to deal with me. So he telephoned to you immediately. He had to get you into Dane's Tower, to take the blame of whatever might be done there. But, probably before you arrived, he found that we were already there. He let you into the cellar beneath us, while he attempted to murder us with Nordensen's Ray. Had he succeeded, you would have been found alone in that deserted tower with our two bodies, and, in view of other circumstances, it is probable that no other murderer would have been thought of but yourself. It is very fortunate that I happened to bring the necessary apparatus for cutting our way out. It seems to have saved your life as well as ours. This formula, as I supposed, is Professor Cheney's. As I had seen it, it was no longer necessary to make a secret of it, so he used it to incriminate you. The plan of the passages, being found on you, would also have been damning evidence against you; but while he was alive I think you would have been unable to escape by the passages. When Kent and I were disposed of, he would have closed the entrance to them, and would have left the way up from the cellar open. You would have been shut in with our bodies, while he made his escape, unseen, and his very existence almost unknown.

"The evidence of his marriage to your daughter remained in his safe, where I found it, and with it other evidence which I have been able to decipher. It proves a depth of villainy beyond what I expected. Not only was Orme the head of a gang of malignant blackmailers but he contemplated a revenge on his country of an even more horrible kind, by the use of several deadly inventions. One of them was a new gas manufactured at V. S. Stephens's works in Barking. It would seem that he was prepared to strike within a few days.

"All this evidence, Channing, if you will come with me, I will now hand over to you. You can then do what is necessary."

We rose to go. Mr. Francis was quite worn out as was indeed natural after his terrible experiences and Forbes courteously helped him to his room.

"As for you, Kent," my friend said when he returned, "you really must have what is left of your interrupted holiday. There will be no eavesdropper now among the rhododendrons at Cheney Park, and Miss Cheney and you, I am sure, will be able to do without me for a very long time to come."

But that is just what Mary and I have determined not to do if we can help it.

THE EDINGTONS
THE HOUSE OF THE
VANISHING
GOBLETS

THE
DESERT LAKE
MYSTERY

KAY CLEAVER STRAHAN
Author of THE DESERT MOON MYSTERY

THE STUDIO
MURDER MYSTERY
THE EDINGTONS

DEATH
ON THE CAMPUS
ADDISON
SIMMONS

COACHWHIP PUBLICATIONS

COACHWHIPBOOKS.COM

Coachwhip Publications
CoachwhipBooks.com

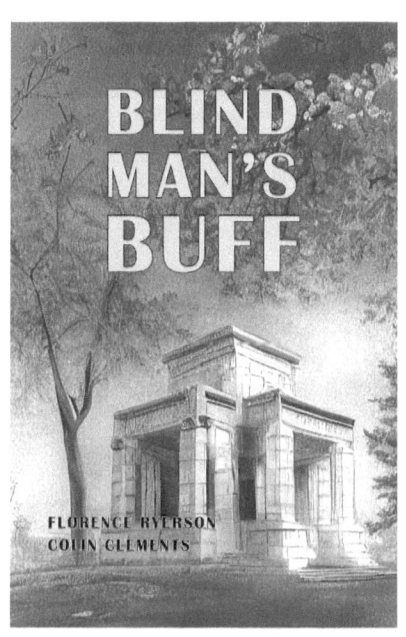

BLIND MAN'S BUFF

FLORENCE RYERSON
COLIN CLEMENTS

POISON CASE
NUMBER 10

MURDER CASE
NUMBER 33

FROM THE FILES OF
THE MICHAEL JOYCE AGENCY

LOUIS CORNELL

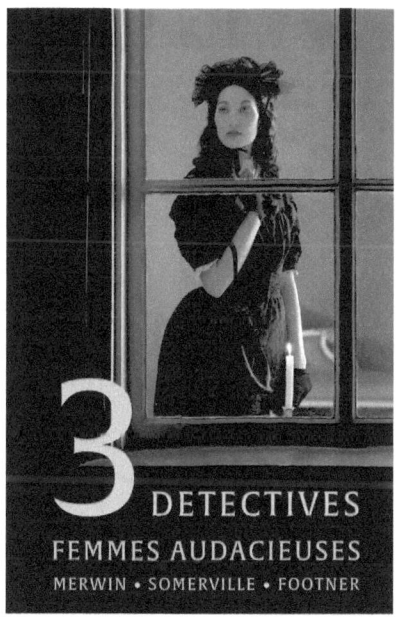

3 DETECTIVES
FEMMES AUDACIEUSES
MERWIN · SOMERVILLE · FOOTNER

MEDORA FIELD

WHO KILLED
AUNT MAGGIE?

COACHWHIP PUBLICATIONS
CoachwhipBooks.com

COACHWHIP PUBLICATIONS

COACHWHIPBOOKS.COM

THE
BEACON HILL
MURDERS
&
THE
BACK BAY
MURDERS

THE ROGER SCARLETT MYSTERIES
VOL. I

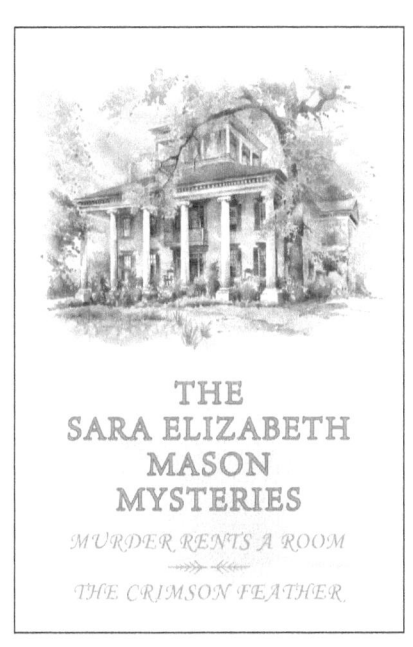

THE
SARA ELIZABETH
MASON
MYSTERIES

MURDER RENTS A ROOM

THE CRIMSON FEATHER

HELEN BURNHAM

THE MURDER OF
LALLA LEE

THE TELLTALE
TELEGRAM

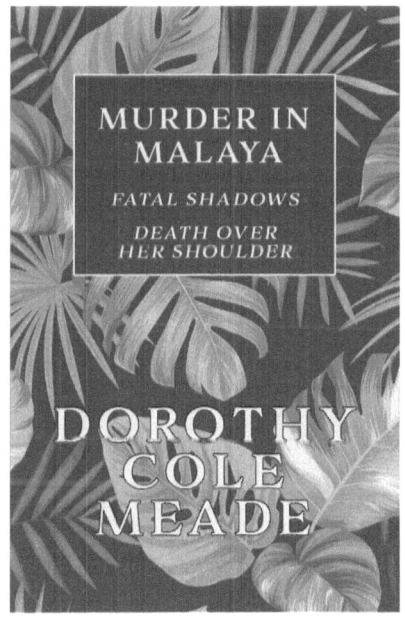

MURDER IN
MALAYA

FATAL SHADOWS

DEATH OVER
HER SHOULDER

DOROTHY
COLE
MEADE

COACHWHIP PUBLICATIONS

CoachwhipBooks.com

THE MYSTERIOUS WAYS
OF WANG FOO

SIDNEY C. PARTRIDGE

MURDER
ON THE
BLUFF

ESTHER TYLER

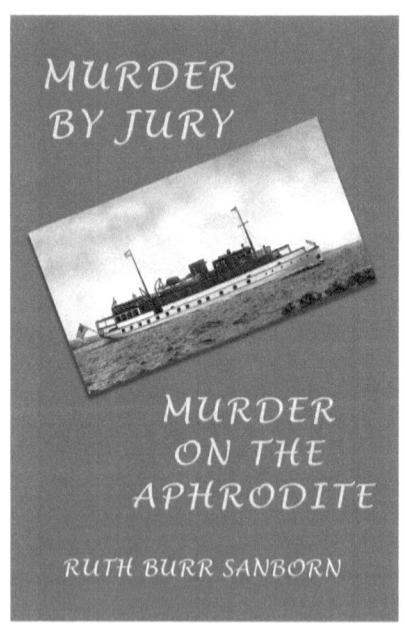

MURDER
BY JURY

MURDER
ON THE
APHRODITE

RUTH BURR SANBORN

LADIES
IN BOXES
GELETT
BURGESS

COACHWHIP PUBLICATIONS
COACHWHIPBOOKS.COM

HIDE AND GO SEEK

with, GOING TO ST. IVES

COLVER HARRIS

A JUDGE MASSIE
MYSTERY

THE CORPSE IS
INDIGNANT

DOUGLAS STAPLETON
and HELEN A. CAREY

hot tip JACK DOLPH

THE SERGEANT HARTY MYSTERIES

JOEL Y. DANE

MURDER CUM LAUDE
1
THE CABANA MURDERS

COACHWHIP PUBLICATIONS

COACHWHIPBOOKS.COM

MURDER AT DRAKE'S ANCHORAGE

E. LEE WADDELL

MAUDE PARKER

MURDER IN JACKSON HOLE

PATTERN IN BLACK AND RED

FARADAY KEENE

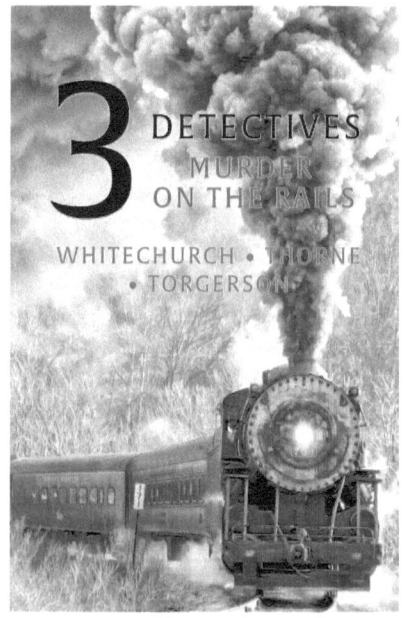

3 DETECTIVES
MURDER ON THE RAILS
WHITECHURCH • THORNE • TORGERSON

COACHWHIP PUBLICATIONS

COACHWHIPBOOKS.COM

THE FIRES AT FITCH'S FOLLY

KENNETH WHIPPLE

MURDER IN STYLE

Emma Lou Fetta

GRIMM DEATH

DEATH COMES TO PERIGORD

JOHN FERGUSON

COACHWHIP PUBLICATIONS

COACHWHIPBOOKS.COM

www.ingramcontent.com/pod-product-compliance
Lightning Source LLC
Chambersburg PA
CBHW020205270626
47157CB00028B/1387